HORRID HENRY RULES THE WORLD

FRANCESCA SIMON

HORRID HENRY RULES THE WORLD

Illustrated by Tony Ross

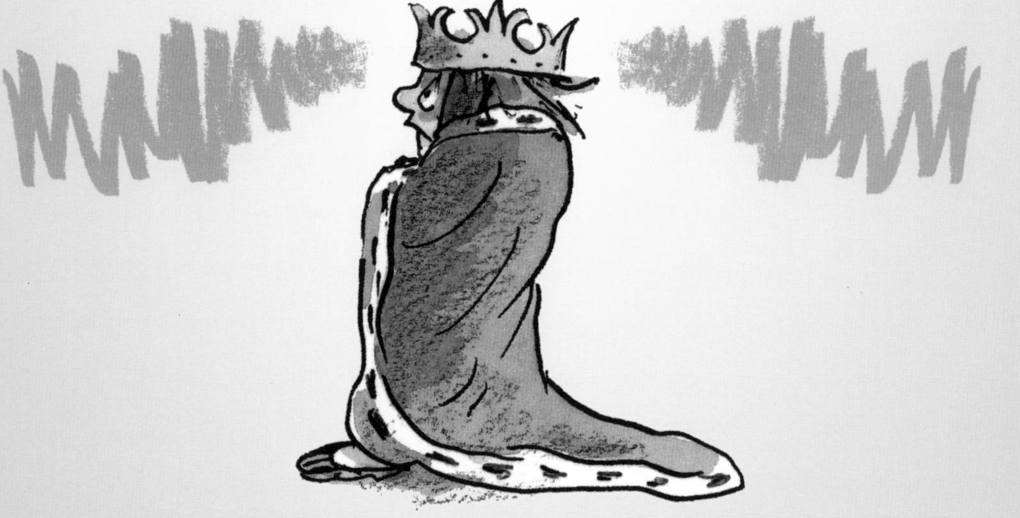

Orion
Children's Books

For Judith Elliott
and Fiona Kennedy,
there at the start

First published in Great Britain in 2007
by Orion Children's Books
a division of the Orion Publishing Group Ltd
Orion House
5 Upper St Martin's Lane
London WC2H 9EA

An Hachette Livre UK Company

1 3 5 7 9 10 8 6 4 2

The Orion Publishing Group's policy is to use papers that
are natural, renewable and recyclable products and made
from wood grown in sustainable forests. The logging and
manufacturing processes are expected to conform to the
environmental regulations of the country of origin.

A catalogue record for this book
is available from the British Library.

ISBN 978 184255 567 5

Printed in Italy by Printer Trento

www.orionbooks.co.uk

CONTENTS

HORRID HENRY'S YEAR BOOK

Our
Christmas
Play

The Queen's
Visit

The Big Football Match

Our School Band

Tidy Monitors

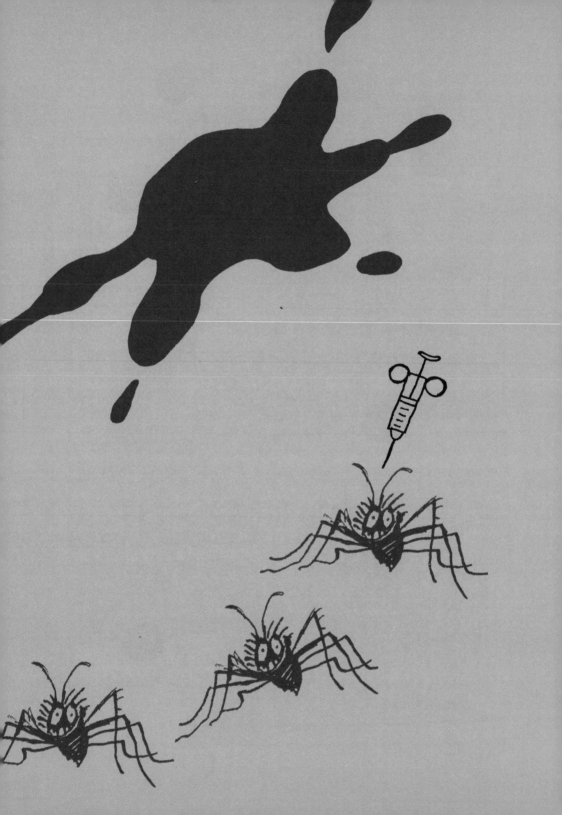

HORRID HENRY'S INJECTION

AaggH!!
AAAAGGGHHHH!!!!
AAAAAGGGGGHHHHH!!!!

The horrible screams came from behind Nurse
Needle's closed door.

Horrid Henry looked at his younger brother
Perfect Peter. Perfect Peter looked at Horrid Henry.
Then they both looked at their father, who
stared straight ahead.

Henry and Peter were in
Dr Dettol's waiting room.

Moody Margaret was there.
So were Sour Susan, Anxious
Andrew, Jolly Josh, Weepy
William, Tough Toby, Lazy
Linda, Clever Clare, Rude
Ralph and just about everyone
Henry knew. They were all waiting for the terrible
moment when Nurse Needle would call their name.

Today was the worst day in the world. Today was –
injection day.

Horrid Henry was not afraid of spiders.

He was not afraid of spooks.

He was not afraid of burglars, bad dreams, squeaky

doors and things that go bump in the night. Only one thing scared him.

Just thinking about . . . about . . . Henry could barely even say the word – INJECTIONS – made him shiver and quiver and shake and quake.

Nurse Needle came into the waiting room.

Henry held his breath.

'Please let it be someone else,' he prayed.

'William!' said Nurse Needle.

Weepy William burst into tears.

'Let's have none of that,' said Nurse Needle. She took him firmly by the arm and closed the door behind him.

'I don't need an injection!' said Henry. 'I feel fine.'

'Injections stop you getting ill,' said Dad. 'Injections fight germs.'

'I don't believe in germs,' said Henry.

11

'I do,' said Dad.

'I do,' said Peter.

'Well, I don't,' said Henry.

Dad sighed. 'You're having an injection, and that's that.'

'I don't mind injections,' said Perfect Peter. 'I know how good they are for me.'

Horrid Henry pretended he was an alien who'd come from outer space to jab earthlings.

'OWW!' shrieked Peter.

'Don't be horrid, Henry!' shouted Dad.

AAAAAAGGGGGHHHHHHH!

came the terrible screams from behind Nurse Needle's door.

AAAAAAGGGGGHHHHHHH!

NOOOOOOOO!

Then Weepy William staggered out, clutching his arm and wailing.

'Crybaby,' said Henry.

'Just wait, Henry,' sobbed William. Nurse Needle came into the waiting room.

Henry closed his eyes.

'Don't pick me,' he begged silently.
'Don't pick me.'

'Susan!' said Nurse Needle.

Sour Susan crept into Nurse Needle's
office.

AAAAAAGGGGGHHHHHH!

came the terrible screams.

AAAAAAGGGGGHHHHHH!
NOOOOOOO!

Then Sour Susan dragged herself out, clutching her
arm and snivelling.

'What a crybaby,' said Henry.

'Well, we all know about *you*, Henry,' said Susan sourly.

'Oh yeah?' said Henry. 'You don't know anything.'

13

Nurse Needle reappeared.

Henry hid his face behind his hands.

I'll be so good if it's not me, he thought. Please, let it be someone else.

'Margaret!' said Nurse Needle.

Henry relaxed.

'Hey, Margaret, did you know the needles are so big and sharp they can go right through your arm?' said Henry.

Moody Margaret ignored him and marched into Nurse Needle's office.

Henry could hardly wait for her terrible screams. Boy, would he tease that crybaby Margaret!

Silence.

Then Moody Margaret swaggered into the waiting room, proudly displaying an enormous plaster on her arm. She smiled at Henry.

'Ooh, Henry, you won't believe the needle she's using today,' said Margaret. 'It's as long as my leg.'

'Shut up, Margaret,' said Henry. He was breathing very fast and felt faint.

'Anything wrong, Henry?' asked Margaret sweetly.

'No,' said Henry. He scowled at her. How dare she not scream and cry?

'Oh, good,' said Margaret. 'I just wanted to warn you because I've never seen such big fat whopping needles in all my life!'

Horrid Henry steadied himself. Today would be different.

He would be brave.

He would be fearless.

He would march into Nurse Needle's office, offer his arm, and dare her to do her worst. Yes, today was the day. Brave Henry, he would be called, the boy who laughed when the needle went in, the boy who asked for a second injection, the boy who –

'Henry!' said Nurse Needle.

'NO!' shrieked Henry. 'Please, please, NO!'

'Yes,' said Nurse Needle. 'It's your turn now.'

Henry forgot he was brave.

Henry forgot he was fearless.

Henry forgot everyone was watching him.

Henry started screaming and screeching and kicking.

'OW!' yelped Dad.

'OW!' yelped Perfect Peter.

'OW!' yelped Lazy Linda.

Then everyone started screaming and screeching.

'I don't want an injection!' shrieked Horrid Henry.

'I don't want an injection!' shrieked Anxious Andrew.

'I don't want an injection!' shrieked Tough Toby.

'Stop it,' said Nurse Needle. 'You need an injection and an injection is what you will get.'

'Him first!' screamed Henry, pointing at Peter.

'You're such a baby, Henry,' said Clever Clare.

That did it.

No one *ever* called Henry a baby and lived.

He kicked Clare as hard as he could. Clare screamed.

Nurse Needle and Dad each grabbed one of Henry's arms and dragged him howling into her office. Peter followed behind, whistling softly.

Henry wriggled free and dashed out. Dad nabbed him and brought him back. Nurse Needle's door clanged shut behind them.

Henry stood in the corner. He was trapped.

Nurse Needle kept her distance. Nurse Needle knew Henry. Last time he'd had an injection he'd kicked her.

Dr Dettol came in.

'What's the trouble, Nurse?' she asked.

'Him,' said Nurse Needle. 'He doesn't want an injection.'

Dr Dettol kept her distance. Dr Dettol knew Henry. Last time he'd had an injection he'd bitten her.

'Take a seat, Henry,' said Dr Dettol.

Henry collapsed in a chair. There was no escape.

'What a fuss over a little thing like an injection,' said Dr Dettol. 'Call me if you need me,' she added, and left the room.

Henry sat on the chair, breathing hard. He tried not

to look as Nurse
Needle examined
her gigantic pile
of syringes.

But he could not
stop himself peeking
through his fingers.
He watched as she got
the injection ready,
choosing the longest,
sharpest, most wicked
needle Henry had ever
seen.

Then Nurse Needle approached, weapon in hand.

'Him first!' shrieked Henry.

Perfect Peter sat down and rolled up his sleeve.

'I'll go first,' said Peter. 'I don't mind.'

'Oh,' he said, as he was jabbed.

'That was perfect,' said Nurse Needle.

'What a good boy you are,' said Dad.

Perfect Peter smiled proudly.

Nurse Needle rearmed herself.

Horrid Henry shrank back in the chair. He looked
around wildly.

Then Henry noticed the row of little medicine
bottles lined up on the counter. Nurse Needle was
filling her syringes from them.

Henry looked closer. The labels read: 'Do NOT give injection if a child is feverish or seems ill.'

Nurse Needle came closer, brandishing the injection. Henry coughed.

And closer. Henry sneezed.

And closer. Henry wheezed and rasped and panted.

Nurse Needle lowered her arm.

'Are you all right, Henry?'

'No,' gasped Henry. 'I'm ill. My chest hurts, my head hurts, my throat hurts.'

Nurse Needle felt his sweaty forehead.

Henry coughed again, a dreadful throaty cough.

'I can't breathe,' he choked. 'Asthma.'

'You don't have asthma, Henry,' said Dad.

'I do, too,' said Henry, gasping for breath.

Nurse Needle frowned.

'He is a little warm,' she said.

'I'm ill,' whispered Henry pathetically. 'I feel terrible.'

Nurse Needle put down her syringe.

'I think you'd better bring him back when he's feeling better,' she said.

'All right,' said Dad. He'd make sure Henry's mother brought him next time.

Henry wheezed and sneezed, moaned and groaned, all the way home. His parents put him straight to bed.

'Oh, Mum,' said Henry, trying to sound as weak as possible. 'Could you bring me some chocolate ice cream to soothe my throat? It really hurts.'

'Of course,' said Mum. 'You poor boy.'

Henry snuggled down in the cool sheets. Ahh, this was the life.

'Oh, Mum,' added Henry, coughing. 'Could you bring up the TV? Just in case my head stops hurting long enough for me to watch?'

'Of course,' said Mum.

Boy, this was great! thought Henry. No injection! No school tomorrow! Supper in bed!

There was a knock on the door. It must be Mum with his ice cream. Henry sat up in bed, then remembered he was ill. He lay back and closed his eyes.

'Come in, Mum,' said Henry hoarsely.

'Hello, Henry.'

Henry opened his eye. It wasn't Mum. It was Dr Dettol.

Henry closed his eyes and had a terrible coughing fit.

'What hurts?' said Dr Dettol.

'Everything,' said Henry. 'My head, my throat, my chest, my eyes, my ears, my back and my legs.'

'Oh dear,' said Dr Dettol.

She took out her stethoscope and listened to Henry's chest. All clear.

She stuck a little stick in his mouth and told him to say 'AAAAAH.' All clear.

She examined his eyes and ears, his back and his legs. Everything seemed fine.

'Well, doctor?' said Mum.

Dr Dettol shook her head. She looked grave.

'He's very ill,' said Dr Dettol. 'There's only one cure.'

'What?' said Mum.

'What?' said Dad.

'An injection!'

NEEDLE CHART

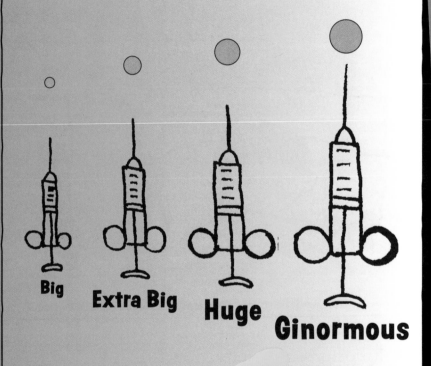

Big

Extra Big

Huge

Ginormous

HORRID HENRY'S SCHOOL FAIR

'Henry! Peter! I need your donations to the school fair NOW!'

Mum was in a bad mood. She was helping Moody Margaret's mum organise the fair and had been nagging Henry for ages to give away some of his old games and toys. Horrid Henry hated giving. He liked getting.

Horrid Henry stood in his bedroom. Everything he owned was on the floor.

'How about giving away those bricks?' said Mum. 'You never play with them any more.'

'NO!' said Henry. They were bound to come in useful some day.

'How about some soft toys? When was the last time you played with Spotty Dog?'

'NO!' said Horrid Henry. 'He's mine!'

Perfect Peter appeared in the doorway dragging two enormous sacks.

'Here's my contribution to the school fair, Mum,' said Perfect Peter.

Mum peeped inside the bags.

'Are you sure you want to give away so many toys?' said Mum.

'Yes,' said Peter. 'I'd like other children to have fun playing with them.'

'What a generous boy you are, Peter,' she said, giving him a big hug.

Henry scowled. Peter could give away all his toys, for all Henry cared. Henry wanted to keep everything.

Wait! How could he have forgotten?

Henry reached under his bed and pulled out a large box hidden under a blanket. The box contained all the useless, horrible presents Henry had ever received. Packs of hankies. Vests with ducks on them. A nature guide. Uggh! Henry hated nature. Why would anyone want to waste their time looking at pictures of flowers and trees?

And then, right at the bottom, was the worst present of all. A Walkie-Talkie-Burpy-Slurpy-Teasy-Weasy Doll. He'd got it for Christmas from a

great-aunt he'd never met. The card she'd written was still attached.

Dear Henrietta
I thought this doll would be perfect for a sweet little two-year-old like you! Take good care of your new baby!
Love
Great-Aunt Greta

Even worse, she'd sent Peter something brilliant.

Dear Pete
You must be a teenager by now and too old for toys, so here's £25. Don't spend it all on sweets!
Love
Great-Aunt Greta

Henry had screamed and begged, but Peter got to keep the money, and Henry was stuck with the doll. He was far too embarrassed to try to sell it, so the doll just lived hidden under his bed with all the other rotten gifts.

'Take that,' said Henry, giving the doll a kick.

'Mama Mama Mama!' burbled the doll. 'Baby burp!'

'Not Great-Aunt Greta's present!' said Mum.

'Take it or leave it,' said Henry. 'You can have the rest as well.'

Mum sighed. 'Some lucky children are going to be very happy.' She took the hateful presents and put them in the jumble sack.

Phew! He'd got rid of that doll at last! He'd lived in terror of Rude Ralph or Moody Margaret coming over and finding it. Now he'd never have to see that burping slurping long-haired thing again.

Henry crept into the spare room where Mum was keeping all the donated toys and games for the fair. He thought he'd have a quick poke around and see what good stuff would be for sale tomorrow. That way he could make a dash and be first in the queue.

There were rolls of raffle tickets, bottles of wine, the barrel for the lucky dip, and sacks and sacks of toys. Wow, what a hoard! Henry just had to move that rolled-up poster out of the way and start rummaging!

Henry pushed aside the poster and then stopped.

I wonder what this is, he thought. I think I'll just unroll it and have a little peek. No harm in that.

Carefully, he untied the ribbon and laid the poster flat on the floor. Then he gasped.

This wasn't jumble. It was the Treasure Map! Whoever guessed where the treasure was hidden always won a fabulous prize. Last year Sour Susan had won a skateboard. The year before Jolly Josh had won a Super Soaker 2000. Boy it sure was worth trying to find that treasure! Horrid Henry usually had at least five goes. But his luck was so bad he had never even come close.

Henry looked at the map. There was the island, with its caves and lagoons, and the sea surrounding it,

filled with whales and sharks and pirate ships. The map was divided into a hundred numbered squares. Somewhere under one of those squares was an X.

I'll just admire the lovely picture, thought Henry. He stared and stared. No X. He ran his hands over the map. No X.

Henry sighed. It was so unfair! He never won anything. And this year the prize was sure to be a Super Soaker 5000.

Henry lifted the map to roll it up. As he raised the thick paper to the light, a large, unmistakable X was suddenly visible beneath square 42.

The treasure was just under the whale's eye.

He had discovered the secret.

'YES!' said Horrid Henry, punching the air. 'It's my lucky day, at last!'

But wait. Mum was in charge of the Treasure Map stall. If he was first in the queue and instantly bagged square 42 she was sure to be suspicious. So how could he let a few other children go first, but make sure none of them chose the right square? And then suddenly, he had a brilliant, spectacular idea . . .

'Tra la la la la!' trilled Horrid Henry, as he, Peter, Mum and Dad walked to the school fair.

'You're cheerful today, Henry,' said Dad.

'I'm feeling lucky,' said Horrid Henry.

He burst into the playground and went straight to the Treasure Map stall. A large queue of eager children keen to pay 20p for a chance to guess had already formed. There was the mystery prize, a large, tempting, Super Soaker-sized box. Wheeee!

Rude Ralph was first in line.

'Psst, Ralph,' whispered Henry. 'I know where X marks the spot. I'll tell you if you give me 50p.'

'Deal,' said Ralph.

'92,' whispered Henry.

'Thanks!' said Ralph. He wrote his name in square 92 and walked off, whistling.

Moody Margaret was next.

'Pssst, Margaret,' whispered Henry. 'I know where X marks the spot.'

'Where?' said Margaret.

'Pay me 50p and I'll tell you,' whispered Henry.

'Why should I trust you?' said Margaret loudly.

Henry shrugged.

'Don't trust me then, and I'll tell Susan,' said Henry.

Margaret gave Henry 50p.

'2,' whispered Horrid Henry.

Margaret wrote her name in square 2, and skipped off.

Henry told Lazy Linda the treasure square was 4.

Henry told Dizzy Dave the treasure square was 100.

Weepy William was told 22.

Anxious Andrew was told 14.

Then Henry thought it was time he bagged the winning square. He made sure none of the children he'd tricked were nearby, then pushed into the queue behind Beefy Bert. His pockets bulged with cash.

'What number do you want, Bert?' asked Henry's mum.

'I dunno,' said Bert.

'Hi Mum,' said Henry. 'Here's my 20p. Hmmm, now where could that treasure be?'

Horrid Henry pretended to study the map.

'I think I'll try 37,' he said. 'No wait, 84. Wait, wait, I'm still deciding...'

'Hurry up Henry,' said Mum. 'Other children want to have a go.'

'Okay, 42,' said Henry.

Mum looked at him. Henry smiled at her and wrote his name in the square.

Then he sauntered off.

He could feel that Super Soaker in his hands already. Wouldn't it be fun to spray the teachers!

Horrid Henry had a fabulous day. He threw wet sponges at Miss Battle-Axe in the 'Biff a Teacher' stall. He joined in his class square dance. He got a marble in the lucky dip. Henry didn't even scream when Perfect Peter won a box of notelets in the raffle and Henry didn't win anything, despite spending £3 on tickets.

TIME TO FIND THE WINNER OF THE TREASURE MAP COMPETITION

boomed a voice over the playground.

Everyone stampeded to the stall.

Suddenly Henry had a terrible thought. What if Mum had switched the X to a different spot at the last minute? He couldn't bear it. He absolutely couldn't bear it. He had to have that Super Soaker!

'And the winning number is . . .' Mum lifted up the Treasure Map . . . '42! The winner is – Henry.'

'Yes!' screamed Henry.

'What?' screamed Rude Ralph, Moody Margaret, Lazy Linda, Weepy William, and Anxious Andrew.

'Here's your prize, Henry,' said Mum.

She handed Henry the enormous box.

'Congratulations.' She did not look very pleased.

Eagerly, Henry tore off the wrapping paper. His prize was a Walkie-Talkie-Burpy-Slurpy-Teasy-Weasy Doll.

'Mama Mama Mama!' burbled the doll. 'Baby Slurp!'

AAARRGGGHHHH!

howled Henry.

Horrid Henry has lost 5 knights, Mr Kill and his Goo-Shooter. Can you find them?

HORRID HENRY'S DANCE CLASS

Stomp stomp stomp
stompstompstompstomp.

Horrid Henry was practising his elephant dance.

Tap tap tap tap tap tap tap tap.

Perfect Peter was practising his raindrop dance. Peter was practising being a raindrop for his dance class show.

Henry was also supposed to be practising being a raindrop. But Henry did not want to be a raindrop. He did not want to be a tomato, a string bean, or a banana either.

Stomp stomp stomp

went Henry's heavy boots.

Tap tap tap

went Peter's tap shoes.

'You're doing it wrong, Henry,' said Peter.

'No I'm not,' said Henry.

'You are too,' said Peter. 'We're supposed to be raindrops.'

Stomp stomp stomp

went Henry's boots. He was an elephant smashing his way through the jungle, trampling on everyone who stood in his way.

'I can't concentrate with you stomping,' said Peter. 'And I have to practise my solo.'

'Who cares?' screamed Horrid Henry. 'I hate dancing, I hate dance class, and most of all, I hate you!'

This was not entirely true. Horrid Henry loved dancing. Henry danced in his bedroom. Henry danced

up and down the stairs. Henry danced on the new sofa
and on the kitchen table.

What Henry hated was having to dance
with other children.

'Couldn't I go to karate instead?' asked
Henry every Saturday.

'No,' said Mum. 'Too violent.'

'Judo?' said Henry.

'N–O spells no,' said Dad.

So every Saturday
morning at 9.45,
Henry and Peter's
father drove them to
Miss Impatience Tutu's
Dance Studio.

Miss Impatience Tutu was skinny and bony. She had long stringy grey hair. Her nose was sharp. Her elbows were pointy. Her knees were wobbly. No one had ever seen her smile.

Perhaps this was because Impatience Tutu hated teaching.

Impatience Tutu hated noise.

Impatience Tutu hated children.

But most of all Impatience Tutu hated Horrid Henry.

This was not surprising. When Miss Tutu shouted, 'Class, lift your left legs,' eleven left legs lifted. One right leg sagged to the floor.

When Miss Tutu screamed, 'Heel, toe, heel, toe,' eleven dainty feet tapped away. One clumpy foot stomped toe, heel, toe, heel.

When Miss Tutu bellowed, 'Class, skip to your right,' eleven bodies turned to the right. One body galumphed to the left.

Naturally, no one wanted to dance with Henry. Or indeed, anywhere near Henry. Today's class, unfortunately, was no different.

'Miss Tutu, Henry is treading on my toes,' said Jolly Josh.

'Miss Tutu, Henry is kicking my legs,' said Lazy Linda.

'Miss Tutu, Henry is bumping me,' said Vain Violet.

'HENRY!' screeched Miss Tutu.

'Yeah,' said Henry.

'I am a patient woman, and you are trying my patience to the limit,' hissed Miss Tutu. 'Any more bad behaviour and you will be very sorry.'

'What will happen?' asked Horrid Henry eagerly.

Miss Tutu stood very tall. She took a long, bony finger and dragged it slowly across her throat.

Henry decided that he would rather live to do battle another day. He stood on the side, gnashing his teeth, pretending he was an enormous crocodile about to gobble up Miss Tutu.

'This is our final rehearsal before the show,' barked Miss Tutu. 'Everything must be perfect.'

Eleven faces stared at Miss Tutu. One face scowled at the floor.

'Tomatoes and beans to the front,' ordered Miss Tutu.

'When Miss Thumper plays the music everyone will

44

stretch out their arms to the
sky, to kiss the morning hello.
Raindrops, stand at the back
next to the giant green leaves
and wait until the beans find the
magic bananas. And Henry,' spat
Miss Tutu, glaring. 'TRY to get
it right.

'Positions, everybody. Miss Thumper,
the opening music please!'
shouted Miss Tutu.
Miss Thumper
banged away.
The tomatoes weaved in
and out, twirling.
The beans pirouetted.
The bananas pointed their
toes and swayed.
The raindrops pitter-patted.

All except one. Henry waved his arms frantically and
raced round the room. Then he crashed into the beans.

'HENRY!' screeched Miss Tutu.

'Yeah,' scowled Henry.

'Sit in the corner!'

Henry was delighted. He sat in the corner and made horrible rude faces while Peter did his raindrop solo.

Tap tap tap tap tap tap tap. Tappa tappa tappa tappa tap tap tap. Tappa tip tappa tip tappa tappa tappa tip.

'Was that perfect, Miss Tutu?' asked Peter.

Miss Tutu sighed. 'Perfect, Peter, as always,' she said, and the corner of her mouth trembled slightly. This was the closest Miss Tutu ever came to smiling.

Then she saw Henry slouching on the chair. Her mouth drooped back into its normal grim position.

Miss Tutu tugged Henry off the chair. She shoved him to the very back of the stage, behind the other raindrops. Then she pushed him behind a giant green leaf.

'Stand there!' shouted Miss Tutu.

'But no one will see me here,' said Henry.

'Precisely,' said Miss Tutu.

It was showtime.

The curtain was about to rise.

The children stood quietly on stage.

Perfect Peter was so excited he almost bounced up and down. Naturally he controlled himself and stood still.

Horrid Henry was not very excited.

He did not want to be a raindrop.

And he certainly did not want to be a raindrop who danced behind a giant green leaf.

Miss Thumper waddled over to the piano. She banged on the keys.

The curtain went up.

Henry's mum and dad were in the audience with the other parents. As usual they sat in the back row, in case they had to make a quick getaway.

They smiled and waved at Peter, standing proudly at the front.

'Can you see Henry?' whispered Henry's mum.

Henry's dad squinted at the stage.

A tuft of red hair stuck up behind the green leaf.

'I think that's him behind the leaf,' said his father doubtfully.

'I wonder why Henry is hiding,' said Mum. 'It's not like him to be shy.'

'Hmmmm,' said Dad.

'Shhh,' hissed the parents beside them.

Henry watched the tomatoes and beans searching on tiptoe for the magic bananas.

I'm not staying back here, he thought, and pushed his way through the raindrops.

'Stop pushing, Henry!' hissed Lazy Linda.

Henry pushed harder, then did a few pitter-pats with the other raindrops.

Miss Tutu stretched out a bony arm and yanked Henry back behind the scenery.

Who wants to be a raindrop anyway, thought Henry. I can do what I like hidden here.

The tomatoes weaved in and out, twirling.

The beans pirouetted.

The bananas pointed their toes and swayed.

The raindrops pitter-patted.

Henry flapped his arms and pretended he was a pterodactyl about to pounce on Miss Tutu.

Round and round he flew, homing in on his prey.

Perfect Peter stepped to the front and began his solo.

Tap tap tap tap

tap tap –

cRASH!

One giant green leaf fell on top of the raindrops, knocking them over.

The raindrops collided with the tomatoes.

The tomatoes smashed into the string beans.

The string beans bumped into the bananas.

Perfect Peter turned his head to see what was happening and danced off the stage into the front row.

Miss Tutu fainted.

The only person still standing on stage was Henry.

Stomp stomp stomp stompstompstompstomp.

Henry did his elephant dance.

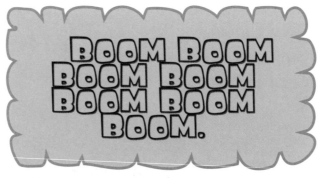

BOOM BOOM
BOOM BOOM
BOOM BOOM
BOOM.

Henry did his buffalo dance.
Peter tried to scramble back on stage.

The curtain fell.

There was a long silence, then Henry's parents clapped.

No one else did, so Henry's parents stopped.

All the other parents ran up to Miss Tutu and started shouting.

'I don't see why that horrid boy should have had such a long solo while all Linda did was lie on the floor,' yelled one mother.

'My Josh is a much better dancer than that boy,' shouted another. 'He should have done the solo.'

'I didn't know you taught modern dance, Miss Tutu,' said Violet's mother. 'Come, Violet,' she added, sweeping from the room.

'HENRY!!' screeched Miss Tutu. 'Leave my dance studio at once!'

'Whoopee!' shouted Henry. He knew that next Saturday he would be at karate class at last.

DON'T MISS THE DANCE EVENT OF THE YEAR!

MISS IMPATIENCE TUTU AND HER TUTURETTES
will be dancing in the world premiere of

THE FARMER'S MARKET

See beans and tomatoes do the Vegetable Waltz!
Marvel at the Plum Fairy and her bevy of cherries.
Ooh and aaah when the mushrooms and radishes whirl and twirl.

BOOK YOUR TICKETS
 NOW!!!

HORRID
HENRY
RULES

HORRID HENRY'S COMPUTER

'**N**o, no, no, no, no!' said Dad.

'No, no, no, no, no!' said Mum.

'The new computer is only for work,' said Dad. 'My work, Mum's work, and school work.'

'Not for playing silly games,' said Mum.

'But everyone plays games on their computer,' said Henry.

'Not in this house,' said Dad. He looked at the computer and frowned. 'Hmmn,' he said. 'How do you turn this thing off?'

'Like this,' said Horrid Henry. He pushed the 'off' button.

'Aha,' said Dad.

It was so unfair! Rude Ralph had *Intergalactic Robot Rebellion*. Dizzy Dave had *Snake Masters Revenge III*.

Kids! *No need to cry when it's time to leave school! Now you can have all the fun of school . . . at home! Take spelling tests! Practise fractions! Learn about the Tudors! It's fun fun fun with . . .*

VIRTUAL CLASSROOM!

Moody Margaret had *Zippy Zappers*. Horrid Henry had *Be a Spelling Champion, Whoopee for Numbers* and *Virtual Classroom*. Aside from Beefy Bert, who'd been given *Counting Made Easy* for Christmas, no one else had such awful software.

'What's the point of finally getting a computer if you can't play games?' said Horrid Henry.

'You can improve your spelling,' said Perfect Peter. 'And write essays. I've already written one for school tomorrow.'

'I don't want to improve my spelling!' screamed Henry. 'I want to play games!'

'I don't,' said Perfect Peter. 'Unless it's *Name that Vegetable* of course.'

'Quite right, Peter,' said Mum.

'You're the meanest parents in the world and I hate you,' shrieked Henry.

'You're the best parents in the world and I love you,' said Perfect Peter.

Horrid Henry had had enough. He leapt on Peter, snarling. He was the Loch Ness monster gobbling up a thrashing duck.

'OWWWWWW!'

squealed Peter.

'Go to your room, Henry!' shouted Dad. 'You're banned from the computer for a week.'

'We'll see about that,' muttered Horrid Henry, slamming his bedroom door.

Snore. Snore. Snore.

Horrid Henry sneaked past Mum and Dad's room and slipped downstairs.

There was the new computer. Henry sat down in front of it and looked longingly at the blank screen.

How could he get some games? He had 53p saved up. Not even enough for *Snake Masters Revenge I*, he thought miserably. Everyone he knew had fun on their computers. Everyone except him. He loved zapping aliens. He loved marshalling armies. He loved ruling the world. But no. His yucky parents would only let him have educational games. Ugh. When he was king anyone who wrote an educational game would be fed to the lions.

Horrid Henry sighed and switched on the computer. Maybe some games were hidden on the hard disk, he thought hopefully. Mum and Dad were scared of computers and wouldn't know how to look.

The word 'Password' flashed up on the screen.

I know a good password, thought Horrid Henry. Quickly he typed in 'Smelly Socks'.

Then Horrid Henry searched. And searched. And searched. But there were no hidden games. Just boring stuff like Mum's spreadsheets and Dad's reports.

Rats, thought Henry. He leaned back in the chair. Would it be fun to switch around some numbers in Mum's dreary spreadsheet? Or add a few words like 'yuck' and 'yah, boo, you're a ninny,' to Dad's stupid report?

Not really.

Wait, what was this? Perfect Peter's homework essay!

Let's see what he's written, thought Henry. Perfect Peter's essay appeared on the screen, titled, 'Why I love my teacher'.

Poor Peter, thought Henry. What a boring title. Let's see if I can improve it for him.

Tap tap tap.

Peter's essay was now called, 'Why I hate my teacher'. That's more like it, thought Henry. He read on.

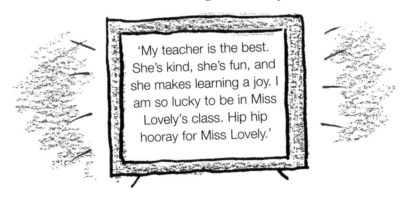

'My teacher is the best. She's kind, she's fun, and she makes learning a joy. I am so lucky to be in Miss Lovely's class. Hip hip hooray for Miss Lovely.'

Oh dear. Worse and worse, thought Horrid Henry.

Tap tap tap.

'My teacher is the worst.' Still missing something, thought Henry.

Tap tap tap.

'My fat teacher is the worst.'

That's more like it, thought Henry. Now for the rest.

Tap tap tap tap tap.

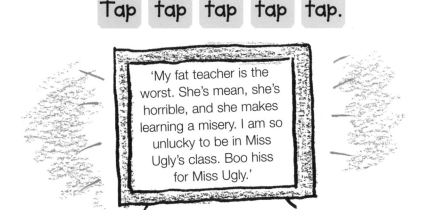

'My fat teacher is the worst. She's mean, she's horrible, and she makes learning a misery. I am so unlucky to be in Miss Ugly's class. Boo hiss for Miss Ugly.'

Much better.

Now that's what I call an essay, thought Horrid Henry. He pressed 'Save', then switched off the computer and tiptoed back to bed.

**ARRRGGHHHH!
AAAHHHH!
NOOOOO!**

Horrid Henry jumped out of bed. Mum was shrieking. Dad was shrieking. Peter was shrieking.

Honestly, couldn't anyone get any rest around here? He stomped down the stairs.

Everyone was gathered round the computer.

'Do something!' shouted Dad. 'I need that report now.'

'I'm trying!' shouted Mum. She pressed a few keys.

'It's jammed,' she said.

'My essay!' wailed Perfect Peter.

'My spreadsheet!' wailed Mum.

'My report!' wailed Dad.

'What's wrong?' said Henry.

'The computer's broken!' said Dad.

'How I hate these horrible machines,' said Mum.

'You've got to fix it,' said Dad. 'I've got to hand in my report this morning.'

'I can't,' said Mum. 'The computer won't let me in.'

'I don't understand,' said Dad. 'We've never needed a password before.'

Suddenly Horrid Henry realised what was wrong. He'd set a new password. No one could use the computer without it. Mum and Dad didn't know anything about passwords. All Horrid Henry had to do to fix the computer was to type in the password 'Smelly Socks.'

'I might be able to help, Dad,' said Horrid Henry.

'Really?' said Dad. He looked doubtful.

'Are you sure?' said Mum. She looked doubtful.

'I'll try,' said Horrid Henry. He sat down in front of the computer. 'Whoops, no I can't,' said Horrid Henry.

'Why not?' said Mum.

'I'm banned,' said Henry. 'Remember?'

'All right, you're unbanned,' said Dad, scowling. 'Just hurry up.'

'I have to be at school with my essay in ten minutes!' moaned Peter.

'And I have to get to work!' moaned Mum.

'I'll do my best,' said Horrid Henry slowly. 'But this is a very hard problem to solve.'

He tapped a few keys and frowned at the screen.

'Do you know what's wrong, Henry?' asked Dad.

'The hard disk is disconnected from the harder disk, and the hardest disk has slipped,' said Horrid Henry.

'Oh,' said Dad.

'Ahh,' said Mum.

'Huunh?' said Perfect Peter.

'You learn about that stuff in computer class next year,' said Horrid Henry. 'Now stand back, everyone, you're making me nervous.'

Mum, Dad, and Peter stepped back.

'You're our last hope, Henry,' said Mum.

'I will fix this on one condition,' said Henry.

'Anything,' said Dad.

'Anything,' said Mum.

'Deal,' said Horrid Henry, and typed in the password.

Whirr! Whirr! Spit!

Horrid Henry scooped up Mum's spreadsheet, Dad's report, and Perfect Peter's essay from the printer and handed them round.

'Thank you so much,' said Dad.

'Thank you so much,' said Mum.

Perfect Peter beamed at his beautifully printed essay, then put it carefully into his school bag. He'd never handed in a printed essay before. He couldn't wait to see what Miss Lovely said.

'Oh my goodness, Peter, what a smart looking essay you've written!' said Miss Lovely.

'It's all about you, Miss Lovely,' said Peter, beaming. 'Would you like to read it?'

'Of course,' said Miss Lovely. 'I'll read it to the class.' She cleared her throat and began:

'Why I ha—' Miss Lovely stopped reading. Her face went pink.

'Peter!' she gasped. 'Go straight to the head! Now!'

'But – but – is it because my essay is so good?' squeaked Peter.

'NO!' said Miss Lovely.

'Waaaaahhh!' wailed Perfect Peter.

PEEEEOWWWW!
BANG!
RAT-A-TAT-TAT!

Another intergalactic robot bit the dust. Now, what shall I play next? thought Horrid Henry happily. *Snake Masters Revenge III*? *Zippy Zapper*? Best of all, Perfect Peter had been banned from the computer for a week,

after Miss Lovely had phoned Mum and Dad to tell them about Peter's rude essay. Peter blamed Henry. Henry blamed the computer.

TO THE MOODIEST MARGARET
Margaret, you old pants face
I've never seen such a nutcase
You are a stinky smelly toad
Won't I laugh when you explode

Ha ha ha to you too, smelly

Stinky

Pongy

Pooey

Whiffy

Odiferous

Odi – what?
Thats not a word.

Is too

Is not

HORRID HENRY
MEETS THE QUEEN

Perfect Peter bowed to himself in the mirror. 'Your Majesty,' he said, pretending to present a bouquet. 'Welcome to our school, your Majesty. My name is Peter, Your Majesty. Thank you, Your Majesty. Goodbye, Your Majesty.' Slowly Perfect Peter retreated backwards, bowing and smiling.

'Oh shut up,' snarled Horrid Henry. He glared at Peter. If Peter said 'Your Majesty' one more time, he would, he would – Horrid Henry wasn't sure what he'd do, but it would be horrible.

The Queen was coming to Henry's school! The real live Queen! The real live Queen, with her dogs and jewels and crowns and castles and beefeaters and knights and horses and ladies-in-waiting, was coming to see the Tudor wall they had built.

Yet for some reason Horrid Henry had not been asked to give the Queen a bouquet. Instead, the head, Mrs Oddbod, had chosen Peter.

Peter!

Why stupid smelly old ugly toad Peter? It was so unfair. Just because Peter had more stars than anyone in the 'Good as Gold' book, was that any reason to choose *him*? Henry should have been chosen. He would do a much better job than Peter. Besides, he wanted to ask the Queen how many TVs she had. Now he'd never get the chance.

'Your Majesty,' said Peter, bowing.

'Your Majesty,' mimicked Henry, curtseying.

Perfect Peter ignored him. He'd been ignoring Henry a lot ever since *he'd* been chosen to meet the queen. Come to think of it, everyone had been ignoring Henry.

'Isn't it thrilling?' said Mum for the millionth time.

'Isn't it fantastic?' said Dad for the billionth time.

'NO!' Henry had said. Who'd want to hand some rotten flowers to a stupid queen anyhow? Not Horrid Henry. And he certainly didn't want to have his picture in the paper, and everyone making a fuss.

'Bow, bouquet, answer her question, walk away,'

muttered Perfect Peter. Then he paused. 'Or is it bouquet, bow?'

Horrid Henry had had just about enough of Peter showing off.

'You're doing it all wrong,' said Henry.

'No I'm not,' said Peter.

'Yes you are,' said Henry. 'You're supposed to hold the bouquet up to her nose, so she can have a sniff before you give it to her.'

Perfect Peter paused.

'No I'm not,' said Peter.

Horrid Henry shook his head sadly. 'I think we'd better practice,' he said. 'Pretend I'm the Queen.' He picked up Peter's shiny silver crown, covered in fool's jewels, and put it on his head.

Perfect Peter beamed. He'd been begging Henry to practise with him all morning. 'Ask me a question the Queen would ask,' said Peter.

Horrid Henry considered.

'Why are you so smelly, little boy?' said the Queen, holding her nose.

'The Queen wouldn't ask *that*!' gasped Perfect Peter.

'Yes she would,' said Henry.

'Wouldn't.'

'Would.'

'And I'm not smelly!'

Horrid Henry waved his hand in front of his face.

'Poo!' said the Queen. 'Take this smelly boy to the Tower.'

'Stop it, Henry,' said Peter. 'Ask me a real question, like my name or what year I'm in.'

'Why are you so ugly?' said the Queen.

'MUM!' wailed Peter. 'Henry called me ugly. And smelly.'

'Don't be horrid, Henry!' shouted Mum.

'Do you want me to practise with you or don't you?' hissed Henry.

'Practise,' sniffed Peter.

'Well, go on then,' said Henry.

Perfect Peter walked up to Henry and bowed.

'Wrong!' said Henry. 'You don't bow to the Queen, you curtsey.'

'Curtsey?' said Peter. Mrs Oddbod hadn't said anything about curtseying. 'But I'm a boy.'

'The law was changed,' said Henry. 'Everyone curtseys now.'

Peter hesitated.

'Are you sure?' asked Peter.

'Yes,' said Henry. 'And when you meet the Queen, you put your thumb on your nose and wriggle your fingers. Like this.'

Horrid Henry cocked a snook.

Perfect Peter gasped. Mrs Oddbod hadn't said anything about thumbs on noses.

'But that's . . . rude,' said Perfect Peter.

'Not to the Queen,' said Horrid Henry. 'You can't just say 'hi' to the Queen like she's a person. She's the Queen. There are special rules. If you get it wrong she can chop off your head.'

Chop off his head! Mrs Oddbod hadn't said anything about chopping off heads.

'That's not true,' said Peter.

'Yes it is,' said Henry.

'Isn't!'

Horrid Henry sighed. 'If you get it wrong, you'll be locked up in the Tower,' he said. 'It's high treason to greet the Queen the wrong way. *Everyone* knows that.'

Perfect Peter paused. Mrs Oddbod hadn't said anything about being locked up in the Tower.

'I don't believe you, Henry,' said Peter.

Henry shrugged.

'Okay. Just don't blame me when you get your head chopped off.'

Come to think of it, thought Peter, there *was* a lot of head-chopping when people met kings and queens. But surely that was just in the olden days . . .

'MUM!' screamed Peter.

Mum ran into the room.

'Henry said I had to curtsey to the Queen,' wailed Peter. 'And that I'd get my head chopped off if I got it wrong.'

Mum glared at Henry.

'How *could* you be so horrid, Henry?' said Mum. 'Go to your room!'

'Fine!' screeched Horrid Henry.

'I'll practise with you, Peter,' said Mum.

'Bow, bouquet, answer her question, walk away,' said Peter, beaming.

The great day arrived. The entire school lined up in the playground, waiting for the Queen. Perfect Peter, dressed in his best party clothes, stood with Mrs Oddbod by the gate.

A large black car pulled up in front of the school.

'There she is!' shrieked the children.

Horrid Henry was furious. Miss Battle-Axe had made him stand in the very last row, as far away from the Queen as he could be. How on earth could he find out if she had 300 TVs standing way back here? Anyone would think Miss Battle-Axe wanted to keep him away from the Queen on purpose, thought Henry, scowling.

Perfect Peter waited, clutching an enormous bouquet of flowers. His big moment was here.

'Bow, bouquet, answer her question, walk away. Bow, bouquet, answer her question, walk away,' mumbled Peter.

'Don't worry, Peter, you'll be perfect,' whispered Mrs Oddbod, urging him forward.

Horrid Henry pushed and shoved to get a closer view. Yes, there was his stupid brother, looking like a worm.

Perfect Peter walked slowly towards the Queen.

'Bow, bouquet, answer her question, walk away,' he mumbled. Suddenly that didn't sound right.

Was it bow, bouquet? Or bouquet, bow?

The Queen looked down at Peter.

Peter looked up at the Queen.

'Your Majesty,' he said.

Now what was he supposed to do next?

Peter's heart began to pound. His mind was blank.

Peter bowed. The bouquet smacked him in the face.

'Oww!' yelped Peter.

What had he practised? Ah yes, now he remembered!

Peter curtseyed. Then he cocked a snook.

Mrs Oddbod gasped.

Oh no, what had he done wrong?

Aaarrgh, the bouquet! It was still in his hand.

Quickly Peter thrust it at the Queen.

Smack!

The flowers hit her in the face.

'How lovely,' said the Queen.

'Waaaa!' wailed Peter. 'Don't chop off my head!'

There was a very long silence. Henry saw his chance.

'How many TVs have you got?' shouted Horrid Henry.

The Queen did not seem to have heard.

'Come along everyone, to the display of Tudor daub-making,' said Mrs Oddbod. She looked a little pale.

'I said,' shouted Henry, 'how many—' A long, bony arm yanked him away.

'Be quiet, Henry,' hissed Miss Battle-Axe. 'Go to the back playground like we practised. I don't want to hear another word out of you.'

Horrid Henry trudged off to the vat of daub with Miss Battle-Axe's beady eyes watching his every step. It was so unfair!

When everyone was in their assigned place, Mrs Oddbod spoke. 'Your Majesty, mums and dads, boys and girls, the Tudors used mud and straw to make daub for their walls. Miss Battle-Axe's class will now show you how.' She nodded to the children standing in the vat. The school recorder band played *Greensleeves*.

Henry's class began to stomp in the vat of mud and straw.

'How lovely,' said the Queen.

Horrid Henry stomped where he'd been placed between Jazzy Jim and Aerobic Al. There was a whole vat of stomping children blocking him from the Queen, who was seated in the front row between Miss Battle-Axe and Mrs Oddbod. If only he could get closer to the Queen. Then he could find out about those TVs!

Henry noticed a tiny space between Brainy Brian and Gorgeous Gurinder.

Henry stomped his way through it.

'Hey!' said Brian.

'Oww!' said Gurinder. 'That was my foot!'

Henry ignored them.

Henry pounded past Greedy Graham and Weepy William.

'Oy!' said Graham. 'Stop pushing.'

'Waaaaaaa!' wept Weepy William.

Halfway to the front!

Henry pushed past Anxious Andrew and Clever Clare.

'Hellllppp!' squeaked Andrew, falling over.

'Watch out, Henry,' snapped Clare.

Almost there! Just Moody Margaret and Jolly Josh stood in his way.

Margaret stomped.

Josh stomped.

Henry trampled through the daub till he stood right behind Margaret.

SQUISH. SQUASH. SQUISH. SQUASH.

'Stop stomping on my bit,' hissed Moody Margaret.

'Stop stomping on *my* bit,' said Horrid Henry.

84

'I was here first,' said Margaret.

'No you weren't,' said Henry. 'Now get out of my way.'

'Make me,' said Moody Margaret.

Henry stomped harder.

SQUELCH! SQUELCH! SQUELCH!

Margaret stomped harder.

STOMP! STOMP! STOMP!

Rude Ralph pushed forward. So did Dizzy Dave.

STOMP! STOMP! STOMP!

Sour Susan pushed forward. So did Kung-Fu Kate.

STOMP! STOMP! STOMP! STOMP! STOMP!

A tidal wave of mud and straw flew out of the vat.

SPLAT!

Miss Battle-Axe was covered.

SPLAT!

Mrs Oddbod was covered.

SPLAT!

The Queen was covered.
'Oops,' said Horrid Henry.
Mrs Oddbod fainted.
'How lovely,' mumbled the Queen.

Buckingham Palace

Dear Mrs Oddbod

The Queen has commanded me to thank you for inviting her to your school to see your lovely display of Tudor daub-making. Enclosed please find a cleaning bill.

Yours sincerely

Hrothgar Frothington

Sir Hrothgar Frothington
Private Secretary to the Queen

CROWN CLEANERS

By Appointment to Her Majesty the Queen

For scrubbing and polishing orb and sceptre	£641.99
For scrubbing and polishing crown	£8,740.08
For dry-cleaning and repairing ermine robes	£12,672.39

Grand total

£22,053.96

**PAYABLE NEXT TUESDAY BY ORDER OF
HER MAJESTY
OR ELSE**

PERFECT PETER'S REVENGE

Perfect Peter had had enough. Why oh why did he always fall for Henry's tricks?

Every time it happened he swore Henry would never ever trick him again. And every time he fell for it. How *could* he have believed that there were fairies at the bottom of the garden? Or that there was such a thing as a Fangmangler? But the time machine was the worst. The very very worst. Everyone had teased him. Even Goody-Goody Gordon asked him if he'd seen any spaceships recently.

Well, never again. His mean, horrible brother had tricked him for the very last time.

I'll get my revenge, thought Perfect Peter, pasting the last of his animal stamps into his album. I'll make Henry sorry for being so mean to me.

But what horrid mean nasty thing could he do? Peter had never tried to be revenged on anyone.

He asked Tidy Ted.

'Mess up his room,' said Ted.

But Henry's room was already a mess.

He asked Spotless Sam.

'Put a spaghetti stain on his shirt,' said Sam.

But Henry's shirts were already stained.

Peter picked up a copy of his favourite magazine *Best Boy*. Maybe it would have some handy hints on the perfect revenge. He searched the table of contents:

BEST BOY

- ❀ Is YOUR bedroom as tidy as it could be?

- ❀ Ten top tips for pleasing your parents

- ❀ How to polish your trophies

- ❀ Why making your bed is good for you

- ❀ Readers tell us about their **FAVOURITE** chores!

Reluctantly, Peter closed *Best Boy* magazine. Somehow he didn't think he'd find the answer inside. He was on his own.

I'll tell Mum that Henry eats sweets in his bedroom, thought Peter. Then Henry would get into trouble. Big big trouble.

But Henry got into trouble all the time. That wouldn't be anything special.

I know, thought Peter, I'll hide Mr Kill. Henry would never admit it, but he couldn't sleep without Mr Kill. But so what if Henry couldn't sleep? He'd just come and jump on Peter's head or sneak downstairs and watch scary movies. I have to think of something really, really horrid, thought Peter. It was hard for Peter to think horrid thoughts, but Peter was determined to try.

He would call Henry a horrid name, like Ugly Toad or Poo Poo face. *That* would show him.

But if I did Henry would hit me, thought Peter. Wait, he could tell everyone at school that Henry wore nappies. Henry the big nappy. Henry the big smelly nappy. Henry nappy face. Henry poopy pants. Peter smiled happily. That would be a perfect revenge.

Then he stopped smiling. Sadly, no one at school would believe that Henry still wore nappies. Worse, they might think that Peter still did! Eeeek.

I've got it, thought Peter, I'll
put a muddy twig in Henry's
bed. Peter had read a great story
about a younger brother who'd done
just that to a mean older one. That would serve Henry
right.

But was a muddy twig enough revenge for all of
Henry's crimes against him?

No it was not.

I give up, thought Peter, sighing. It was hopeless. He
just couldn't think of anything horrid enough.

Peter sat down on his beautifully made bed and
opened *Best Boy* magazine.

TELL MUM HOW MUCH
YOU LOVE HER!

shrieked the headline.

And then a dreadful thought tiptoed into his head.
It was so dreadful, and so horrid, that Perfect Peter
could not believe that he had thought it.

'No,' he gasped. 'I couldn't.' That was too evil.

But . . . but . . . wasn't that exactly what he wanted?
A horrid revenge on a horrid brother?

'Don't do it!' begged his angel.

'Do it!' urged his devil, thrilled to get the chance to speak. 'Go on, Peter! Henry deserves it.'

YES! thought Peter. He would do it. He would be revenged!

Perfect Peter sat down at the computer.

Tap tap tap.

Dear Margaret,
I love you. Will
you marry me?

Peter printed out the note and carefully scrawled:

Henry

There! thought Peter proudly. That looks just like Henry's writing. He folded the note, then sneaked into the garden, climbed over the wall, and left it on the table inside Moody Margaret's Secret Club tent.

'Of course Henry loves me,' said Moody Margaret, preening. 'He can't help it. Everyone loves me because I'm so lovable.'

'No you're not,' said Sour Susan. 'You're moody. And you're mean.'

'Am not!'

'Are too!'

'Am not. You're just jealous 'cause no one would *ever* want to marry you,' snapped Margaret.

'I am not jealous. Anyway, Henry likes *me* the best,' said Susan, waving a folded piece of paper.

'Says who?'

'Says Henry.'

Margaret snatched the paper from Susan's hand and read:

to the Beautiful Susan

Oh Susan,
No one is as pretty as you,
You always smell lovely
Just like shampoo.

Henry

Margaret sniffed. 'Just like dog poo, you mean.'

'I do not,' shrieked Susan.

'Is this your idea of a joke?' snorted Moody Margaret, crumpling the poem.

Sour Susan was outraged.

'No. It was waiting for me on the clubhouse table.

You're just jealous because Henry didn't write *you* a poem.'

'Huh,' said Margaret. Well, she'd show Henry. No one made a fool of her.

Margaret snatched up a pen and scribbled a reply to Henry's note.

'Take this to Henry and report straight back,' she ordered. 'I'll wait here for Linda and Gurinder.'

'Take it yourself,' said Susan sourly. Why oh why was she friends with such a mean, moody jealous grump?

Horrid Henry was inside the Purple Hand Fort plotting death to the Secret Club and scoffing biscuits when an enemy agent peered through the entrance.

'Guard!' shrieked Henry.

But that miserable worm toad was nowhere to be found.

Henry reminded himself to sack Peter immediately.

'Halt! Who goes there?'

'I have an important message,' said the Enemy.

'Make it snappy,' said Henry. 'I'm busy.'

Susan crept beneath the branches.

'Do you really like my shampoo, Henry?' she asked.

Henry stared at Susan. She had a sick smile on her face, as if her stomach hurt.

'Huh?' said Henry.

'You know, my *shampoo*,' said Susan, simpering.

Had Susan finally gone mad?

'*That's* your message?' said Horrid Henry.

'No,' said Susan, scowling. She tossed a scrunched-up piece of paper at Henry and marched off.

Henry opened the note:

I wouldn't marry you if you were the last creature on earth and that includes slimy toads and rattlesnakes. So there.

Margaret

Henry choked on his biscuit. Marry Margaret?!
He'd rather walk around town carrying a Walkie-
Talkie-Burpy-Slurpy-Teasy-Weasy Doll. He'd rather
learn long division. He'd rather trade all his computer
games for a Princess Pamper Parlour. He'd rather . . .
he'd rather . . . he'd rather marry Miss Battle-Axe than
marry Margaret!

What on earth had given Margaret the crazy,
horrible, revolting idea he wanted to marry *her*?

He always knew Margaret was nuts. Now he had
proof. Well well well, thought Horrid Henry gleefully.
Wouldn't he tease her! Margaret would never live this
down.

Henry leapt over the wall and burst into the Secret
Club Tent.

'Margaret, you old pants face, I wouldn't marry you if –'

'Henry loves Margaret! Henry loves Margaret!' chanted Gorgeous Gurinder.

'Henry loves Margaret! Henry loves Margaret!' chanted Lazy Linda, making horrible kissing sounds.

Henry tried to speak. He opened his mouth. Then he closed it.

'No I don't,' gasped Horrid Henry.

'Oh yeah?' said Gurinder.

'Yeah,' said Henry.

'Then why'd you send her a note saying you did?'

'I didn't!' howled Henry.

'And you sent Susan a poem!' said Linda.

'I DID NOT!' howled Henry even louder. What on earth was going on? He took a step backwards.

The Secret Club members advanced on him, shrieking, 'Henry loves Margaret, Henry loves Margaret.'

Time, thought Horrid Henry, to beat a strategic retreat. He dashed back to his fort, the terrible words 'Henry loves Margaret' burning his ears.

'PETER!' bellowed Horrid Henry. 'Come here this minute!'

Perfect Peter crept out of the house to the fort. Henry had found out about the note and the poem. He was dead.

Goodbye, cruel world, thought Peter.

'Did you see anyone going into the Secret Club carrying a note?' demanded Henry, glaring.

Perfect Peter's heart began to beat again.

'No,' said Peter. That wasn't a lie because he hadn't seen himself.

'I want you to stand guard by the wall, and report anyone suspicious to me at once,' said Henry.

'Why?' said Peter innocently.

'None of your business, worm,' snapped Henry. 'Just do as you're told.'

'Yes, Lord High Excellent Majesty of the Purple Hand,' said Perfect Peter. What a lucky escape!

Henry sat on his Purple Hand throne and considered. Who was this foul fiend? Who was this evil genius? Who was spreading these foul rumours? He had to find out, then strike back hard before the snake struck again.

But who'd want to be his enemy? He was such a nice, kind, friendly boy.

True, Rude Ralph wasn't very happy when Henry called him Ralphie Walfie.

Tough Toby wasn't too pleased when Henry debagged him during playtime.

And for some reason, Brainy Brian didn't see the joke when Henry scribbled all over his book report.

Vain Violet said she'd pay Henry back for pulling her pigtails.

And just the other day Fiery Fiona said Henry would be sorry he'd laughed during her speech in assembly.

Even Kind Kasim warned Henry to stop being so horrid or he'd teach him a lesson he wouldn't forget.

But maybe Margaret was behind the whole plot. He had stinkbombed her Secret Club, after all.

Hmmn. The list of suspects was rather long.

It had to be Ralph. Ralph loved playing practical jokes.

Well, it's not funny, Ralph, thought Horrid Henry. Let's see how *you* like it. Perhaps a little poem to Miss Battle-Axe . . .

Horrid Henry grabbed a piece of paper and began to scribble:

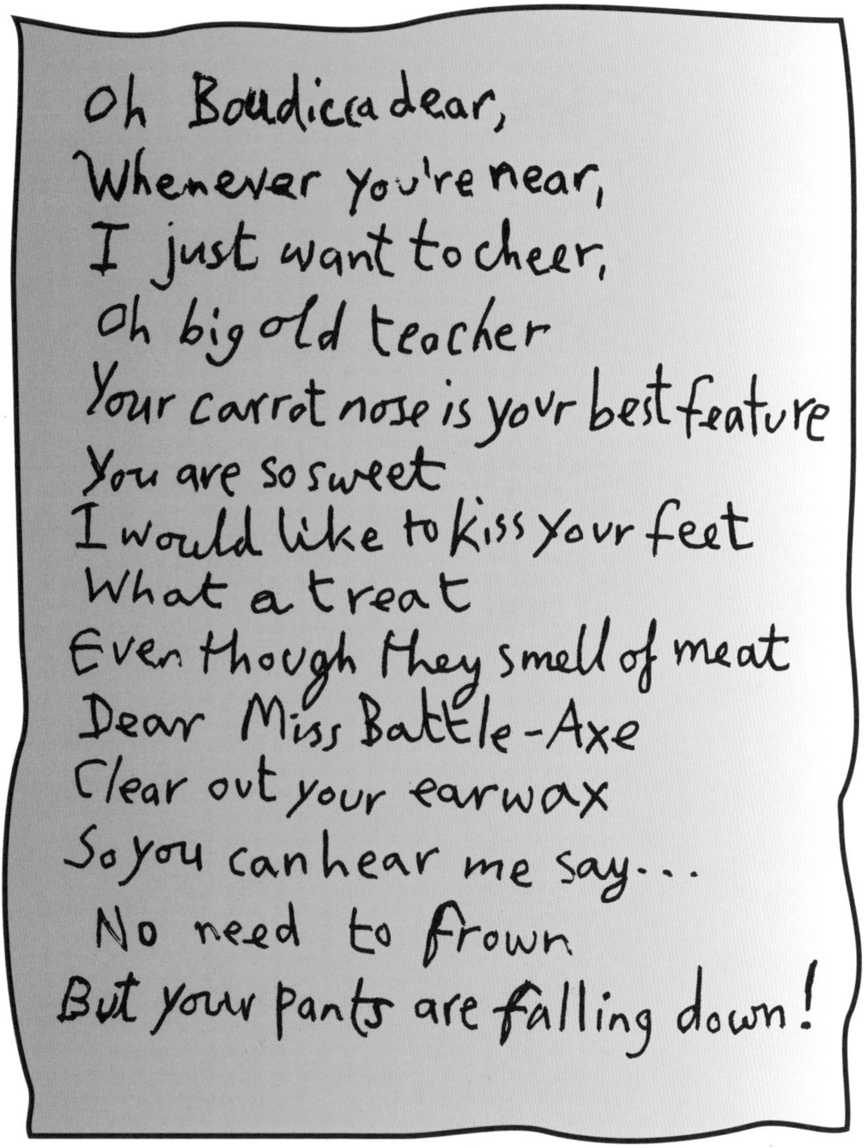

Oh Boudicca dear,
Whenever you're near,
I just want to cheer,
Oh big old teacher
Your carrot nose is your best feature
You are so sweet
I would like to kiss your feet
What a treat
Even though they smell of meat
Dear Miss Battle-Axe
Clear out your earwax
So you can hear me say...
No need to frown
But your pants are falling down!

Ha ha ha ha ha, thought Henry. He'd sign the poem 'Ralph', get to school early and pin the poem on the door of the Girls' Toilet. Ralph would get into big big trouble.

But wait.

What if Ralph *wasn't* responsible? Could it be Toby after all? Or Margaret? There was only one thing to do.

Henry copied his poem seven times, signing each copy with a different name. He would post them all over school tomorrow. One of them was sure to be guilty.

Henry sneaked into school, then quickly pinned up his poems on every noticeboard. That done, he swaggered onto the playground. Revenge is sweet, thought Horrid Henry.

There was a crowd gathered outside the boys' toilets. 'What's going on?' shrieked Horrid Henry, pushing

and shoving his way through the crowd.

'Henry loves Margaret,' chanted Tough Toby.

'Henry loves Margaret,' chanted Rude Ralph.

Uh oh.

Henry glanced at the toilet door. There was a note taped on it.

Dear Margaret
I love you.
Will you marry me?
Henry

Henry's blood froze. He ripped the note off the door.

'Margaret wrote it to herself,' blustered Horrid Henry.

'Didn't!' said Margaret.

'Did!' said Henry.

'Besides, you love *me*!' shrieked Susan.

'No I don't!' shrieked Henry.

'That's 'cause you love me!' said Margaret.

'I hate you!' shouted Henry.

'I hate you more!' said Margaret.

'I hate *you* more,' said Henry.

'You started it,' said Margaret.

'Didn't.'

'Did! You asked me to marry you.'

'NO WAY!' shrieked Henry.

'And you sent me a poem!' said Susan.

'No I didn't!' howled Henry.

'Well, if you didn't then who did?' said Margaret.

Silence.

'Henry,' came a little voice, 'can we play pirates after school today?'

Horrid Henry thought an incredible thought.

Moody Margaret thought an incredible thought.

Sour Susan thought an incredible thought.

Three pairs of eyes stared at Perfect Peter.

'Wha . . . what?' said Peter.

Uh oh.

'HELP!' shrieked Perfect Peter. He turned and ran.

AAAARRRRGHHHHHH!

shrieked Horrid Henry, chasing after him. 'You're dead meat, worm!'

Miss Battle-Axe marched onto the playground. She was clutching a sheaf of papers in her hand.

'Margaret! Brian! Ralph! Toby! Violet! Kasim! Fiona! What is the meaning of these poems? Straight to the head – now!'

Perfect Peter crashed into her.

Smash!

Miss Battle-Axe toppled backwards into the bin. 'And you too, Peter,' gasped Miss Battle-Axe.

Waaaaaaa!

wailed Perfect Peter. From now on, he'd definitely be sticking to good deeds. Whoever said revenge was sweet didn't have a horrid brother like Henry.

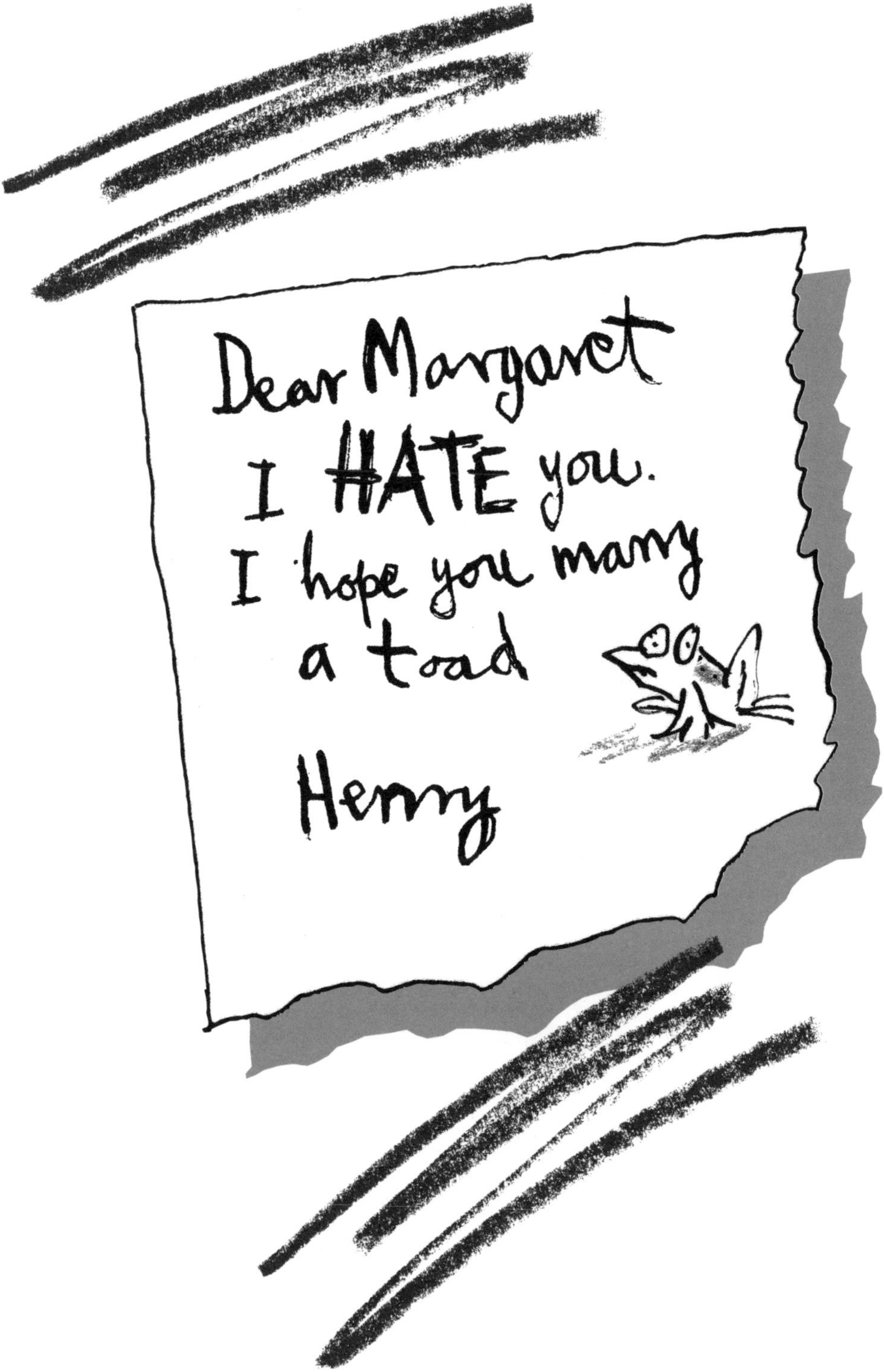
Dear Margaret
I HATE you.
I hope you marry a toad
Henry

HORRID HENRY
AND THE
FOOTBALL FIEND

'A . . . ND with 15 seconds to go it's Hot-Foot Henry racing across the pitch! Rooney tries a slide tackle but Henry's too quick! Just look at that step-over! Oh no, he can't score from that distance, it's crazy, it's impossible, oh my goodness, he cornered the ball, it's IN!!!! It's IN! Another *spectacular* goal! Another spectacular win! And it's all thanks to Hot-Foot Henry, the greatest footballer who's ever lived!'

'Goal! Goal! Goal!' roared the crowd. Hot-Foot Henry had won the match! His teammates carried him through the fans, cheering and chanting, 'Hen-ry! Hen-ry! Hen-ry!'

'HENRY!'

Horrid Henry looked up to see Miss Battle-Axe leaning over his table and glaring at him with her red eyes.

'What did I just say?'

'Henry,' said Horrid Henry.

Miss Battle-Axe scowled.

'I'm watching you, Henry,' she snapped. 'Now class, please pay attention, we need to discuss—'

'Waaaaa!' wailed Weepy William. 'Susan, stop pulling my hair!' squealed Vain Violet.

'Miss!' shouted Inky Ian, 'Ralph's snatched my pen!'

'Didn't!' shouted Rude Ralph.

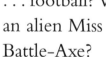

'Did!' shouted Inky Ian.

'Class! Be quiet!' bellowed Miss Battle-Axe.

'Waaaaa!' wailed Weepy William.

'Owwww!' squealed Vain Violet.

'Give it back!' shouted Inky Ian.

'Fine,' said Miss Battle-Axe, 'we won't talk about football.'

William stopped wailing.

Violet stopped squealing.

Ian stopped shouting.

Henry stopped daydreaming.

Everyone in the class stared at Miss Battle-Axe. Miss Battle-Axe wanted to talk about
. . . football? Was this
an alien Miss
Battle-Axe?

'As you all know, our local team, Ashton Athletic, has reached the sixth round of the FA Cup,' said Miss Battle-Axe.

'YEY!' shrieked the class.

'And I'm sure you all know what happened last night . . .'

Last night! Henry could still hear the announcer's glorious words as he and Peter had gathered round the radio as the draw for round six was announced.

'Number 16, Ashton Athletic, will be playing . . .' there was a long pause as the announcer drew another ball from the hat . . . 'number 7, Manchester United.'

'Go Ashton!' shrieked Horrid Henry.

'As I was saying, before I was so rudely interrupted—' Miss Battle-Axe glared at Horrid Henry, 'Ashton are playing Manchester United in a few weeks. Every local primary school has been given a pair of tickets. And thanks to my good luck in the teacher's draw, the lucky winner will come from our class.'

'Me!' screamed Horrid Henry.

'Me!' screamed Moody Margaret.

'Me!' screamed Tough Toby, Aerobic Al, Fiery Fiona and Brainy Brian.

'No one who shouts out will be getting anything,' said Miss Battle-Axe. 'Our class will be playing a football match at lunchtime. The player of the match will win the tickets. I'm the referee and my decision will be final.'

Horrid Henry was so stunned that for a moment he could scarcely breathe. FA Cup tickets! FA Cup tickets to see his local team Ashton play against Man U! Those tickets were like gold dust. Henry had begged and pleaded with Mum and Dad to get tickets, but naturally they were all sold out by the time Henry's mean, horrible, lazy parents managed to heave their stupid bones to the phone. And now here was another chance to go to the match of the century!

Ashton Athletic had never got so far in the Cup. Sure, they'd knocked out the Tooting Tigers (chant: Toot Toot! Grrr!) the Pynchley Pythons and the Cheam Champions but—Manchester United! Henry had to go to the game. He just had to. And all he had to do was be man of the match.

There was just one problem. Unfortunately, the best footballer in the class wasn't Horrid Henry. Or Aerobic Al. Or Beefy Bert.

The best footballer in the class was Moody Margaret.

117

The second best player in the class was Moody Margaret. The third best player in the class was Moody Margaret. It was so unfair! Why should Margaret of all people be so fantastic at football?

Horrid Henry was brilliant at shirt pulling. Horrid Henry was superb at screaming 'Offside!' (whatever that meant). No one could howl 'Come on, ref!' louder.

And at toe-treading, elbowing, barging, pushing, shoving and tripping, Horrid Henry had no equal. The only thing Horrid Henry wasn't good at was playing football.

But never mind. Today would be different. Today he would dig deep inside and find the power to be Hot-Foot Henry—for real. Today no one would stop him. FA Cup match here I come, thought Horrid Henry gleefully.

Lunchtime!

Horrid Henry's class dashed to the back play-ground, where the pitch was set up. Two jumpers either end marked the goals. A few parents gathered on the sidelines.

Miss Battle-Axe split the class into two teams: Aerobic Al was captain of Henry's team, Moody Margaret was captain of the other.

There she stood in midfield, having nabbed a striker position, smirking confidently. Horrid Henry glared at her from the depths of the outfield.

'Na na ne nah nah, I'm sure to be man of the match,' trilled Moody Margaret, sticking out her tongue at him. 'And you-ooo won't.'

'Shut up, Margaret,' said Henry. When he was king,

anyone named Margaret would be boiled in oil and
fed to the crows.

'Will you take me to the match, Margaret?' said
Susan. 'After all, *I'm* your best friend.'

Moody Margaret scowled. 'Since when?'

'Since always!' wailed Susan.

'Huh!' said Margaret. 'We'll just have to see how
nice you are to me, won't we?'

'Take me,' begged Brainy Brian. 'Remember how I
helped you with those fractions?'

'And called me stupid,' said Margaret.

'Didn't,' said Brian.

'Did,' said Margaret.

Horrid Henry eyed his classmates. Everyone looking
straight ahead, everyone determined to be man of the

match. Well, wouldn't they be in for a shock when Horrid Henry waltzed off with those tickets!

'Go Margaret!' screeched Moody Margaret's mum.

'Go Al!' screeched Aerobic Al's dad.

'Everyone ready?' said Miss Battle-Axe. 'Bert! Which team are you on?'

'I dunno,' said Beefy Bert.

Miss Battle-Axe blew her whistle.

Kick

Dribble

Dribble

Pass

Kick

Save!

Goal Kick

Henry stood disconsolately on the left wing, running back and forth as the play passed him by. How could he ever be man of the match stuck out here? Well, no way was he staying in this stupid spot a moment longer.

Horrid Henry abandoned his position and chased after the ball. All the other defenders followed him.

Moody Margaret had the ball. Horrid Henry ran up behind her. He glanced at Miss Battle-Axe. She was busy chatting to Mrs Oddbod. Horrid Henry went for a two foot slide tackle and tripped her.

'Foul!' screeched Margaret. 'He hacked my leg!'

'Liar!' screeched Henry. 'I just went for the ball!'

'Cheater!' screamed Moody Margaret's mum.

'Play on,' ordered Miss Battle-Axe.

Yes! thought Horrid Henry triumphantly. After all, what did blind old Miss Battle-Axe know about the rules of football? Nothing. This was his golden chance to score.

Now Jazzy Jim had the ball.

Horrid Henry trod on his toes, elbowed him, and grabbed the ball.

'Hey, we're on the same team!' yelped Jim.

Horrid Henry kept dribbling.

'Pass! Pass!' screamed Al. 'Man on!'

Henry ignored him. Pass the ball? Was Al mad? For once Henry had the ball and he was keeping it.

Then suddenly Moody Margaret appeared from behind, barged him, dribbled the ball past Henry's team and kicked it straight past Weepy William into goal. Moody Margaret's team cheered.

Weepy William burst into tears.
'Waaaaaa,' wailed Weepy William.
'Idiot!' screamed Aerobic Al's dad.
'She cheated!' shrieked Henry. 'She fouled me!'
'Didn't,' said Margaret.

'How dare you call my daughter a cheater?' screamed Margaret's mum.

Miss Battle-Axe blew her whistle.

'Goal to Margaret's team. The score is one-nil.'

Horrid Henry gritted his teeth. He would score a goal if he had to trample on every player to do so.

Unfortunately, everyone else seemed to have the same idea.

'Ralph pushed me!' shrieked Aerobic Al.

'Didn't!' lied Rude Ralph. 'It was just a barge.'

'He used his hands, I saw him!' howled Al's father. 'Send him off.'

'I'll send *you* off if you don't behave,' snapped Miss Battle-Axe, looking up and blowing her whistle.

'It was kept in!' protested Henry.

'No way!' shouted Margaret. 'It went past the line!'

'That was ball to hand!' yelled Kind Kasim.

'No way!' screamed Aerobic Al. 'I just went for the ball.'

'Liar!'

'Liar!'

'Free kick to Margaret's team,' said Miss Battle-Axe.

'Ouch!' screamed Soraya, as Brian stepped on her toes, grabbed the ball, and headed it into goal past Kasim.

'Hurray!' cheered Al's team.

'Foul!' screamed Margaret's team.

'Score is one all,' said Miss Battle-Axe. 'Five more minutes to go.'

AAARRRGGHH!

thought Horrid Henry. I've got to score a goal to have a chance to be man of the match. I've just got to. But how, how?

Henry glanced at Miss Battle-Axe. She appeared to be rummaging in her handbag. Henry saw his chance. He stuck out his foot as Margaret hurtled past.

CRASH!

Margaret tumbled.
Henry seized the ball.

'Henry hacked my leg!' shrieked Margaret.

'Did not!' shrieked Henry. 'I just went for the ball.'

'REF!' screamed Margaret.

'He cheated!' screamed Margaret's mum. 'Are you blind, ref?'

Miss Battle-Axe glared.

'My eyesight is perfect, thank you,' she snapped.

Tee hee, chortled Horrid Henry.

Henry trod on Brian's toes, elbowed him, then grabbed the ball. Then Dave elbowed Henry, Ralph trod on Dave's toes, and Susan seized the ball and kicked it high overhead.

Henry looked up. The ball was high, high up. He'd never reach it, not unless, unless— Henry glanced at

Miss Battle-Axe. She was watching a traffic warden patrolling outside the school gate. Henry leapt into the air and whacked the ball with his hand.

THWACK!

The ball hurled across the goal.

'Goal!' screamed Henry.

'He used his hands!' protested Margaret.

'No way!' shouted Henry. 'It was the hand of God!'

'Hen-ry! Hen-ry! Hen-ry!' cheered his team.

'Unfair!' howled Margaret's team.

Miss Battle-Axe blew her whistle.

'Time!' she bellowed. 'Al's team wins 2-1.'

'Yes!' shrieked Horrid Henry, punching the air. He'd scored the winning goal! He'd be man of the match! Ashton Athletic versus Man U here I come!

Horrid Henry's class limped through the door and sat down. Horrid Henry sat at the front, beaming. Miss Battle-Axe had to award him the tickets after his brilliant performance and spectacular, game-winning goal. The question was, who *deserved* to be his guest?

No one.

I know, thought Horrid Henry, I'll sell my other ticket. Bet I get a million pounds for it. No, a billion pounds. Then I'll buy my own team, and play striker any time I want to. Horrid Henry smiled happily.

Miss Battle-Axe glared at her class.

'That was absolutely disgraceful,' she said. 'Cheating! Moving the goals! Shirt tugging!' she glared at Graham. 'Barging!

She glowered at Ralph. 'Pushing and shoving! Bad sportsmanship!' Her eyes swept over the class.

Horrid Henry sank lower in his seat.

Oops.

'And don't get me started about offside,' she snapped.

Horrid Henry sank even lower.

'There was only one person who deserves to be

player of the match,' she continued. 'One person who observed the rules of the beautiful game. One person who has nothing to be ashamed of today.'

Horrid Henry's heart leapt. *He* certainly had nothing to be ashamed of.

'. . . One person who can truly be proud of their performance . . .'

Horrid Henry beamed with pride.

'And that person is—'

'Me! screamed Moody Margaret.

'Me!' screamed Aerobic Al.

'Me! screamed Horrid Henry.

'—the referee,' said Miss Battle-Axe.

What?

Miss Battle-Axe . . . man of the match?

Miss Battle-Axe . . . a football fiend?

'IT'S NOT FAIR!' screamed the class.

'IT'S NOT FAIR!' screamed Horrid Henry.

HORRID HENRY'S SICK DAY

Cough! Cough! Sneeze! Sneeze!

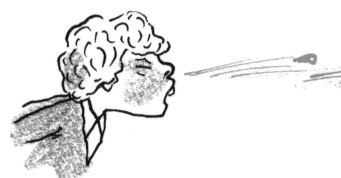

'Are you all right, Peter?' asked Mum.

Peter coughed, choked, and spluttered.

'I'm OK,' he gasped.

'Are you sure?' said Dad. 'You don't look very well.'

'It's nothing,' said Perfect Peter, coughing.

Mum felt Peter's sweaty brow.

'You've got a temperature,' said Mum. 'I think you'd better stay home from school today.'

'But I don't want to miss school,' said Peter.

'Go back to bed,' said Mum.

'But I want to go to school,' wailed Peter. 'I'm sure I'll be—' Peter's pale, sweaty face turned green. He dashed up the stairs to the loo. Mum ran after him.

Bleeeeeeecchhhh

The horrible sound of vomiting filled the house.

Horrid Henry stopped eating his toast. Peter, stay at home? Peter, miss school? Peter, laze about watching TV while he, Henry, had to suffer a long hard day with Miss Battle-Axe?

No way! He was sick, too. Hadn't he coughed twice this morning? And he had definitely sneezed last night. Now that he thought about it, he could feel those flu germs invading. Yup, there they were, marching down his throat.

Stomp stomp stomp marched the germs. Mercy! shrieked his throat. Ha ha ha gloated the germs.

Horrid Henry thought about those spelling words he hadn't learnt. The map he hadn't finished colouring. The book report he hadn't done.

Oww. His throat hurt.

Oooh. His tummy hurt.

Eeek. His head hurt.

Yippee! He was sick!

So what would it be?

Maths or Mutant Max?

Reading or relaxing?

Commas or comics?

Tests or TV?

Hmmm, thought Horrid Henry. Hard choice.

COUGH. COUGH.

Dad continued reading the paper.

**COUGH! COUGH! COUGH!
COUGH! COUGH!**

'Are you all right, Henry?' asked Dad, without looking up.

'No!' gasped Henry. 'I'm sick, too. I can't go to school.'

Slowly Dad put down his newspaper.

'You don't look ill, Henry,' said Dad.

'But I am,' whimpered Horrid Henry. He clutched his throat. 'My throat really hurts,' he moaned. Then he added a few coughs, just in case.

'I feel weak,' he groaned. 'Everything aches.'

Dad sighed.

'All right, you can stay home,' he said.

Yes! thought Horrid Henry. He was amazed. It usually took much more moaning and groaning before his mean, horrible parents decided he was sick enough to miss a day of school.

'But no playing on the computer,' said Dad. 'If you're sick, you have to lie down.'

Horrid Henry was outraged.

'But it makes me feel better to play on the computer,' he protested.

'If you're well enough to play on the computer, you're well enough to go to school,' said Dad.

Rats.

Oh well, thought Horrid Henry. He'd get his duvet, lie on the sofa and watch loads of TV instead. Then Mum would bring him cold drinks, lunch on a tray, maybe even ice cream. It was always such a waste when you were too sick to enjoy being sick, thought Horrid Henry happily.

He could hear Mum and Dad arguing upstairs.

'I need to go to work,' said Mum.

'I need to go to work,' said Dad.

'I stayed home last time,' said Mum.

'No you didn't, I did,' said Dad.

'Are you sure?' said Mum.

'Yes,' said Dad.

'Are you sure you're sure?' said Mum.

Horrid Henry could hardly believe his ears. Imagine arguing over who got to stay home! When he was grown-up he was going to stay home full time, testing computer games for a million pounds a week.

He bounced into the sitting room. Then he stopped bouncing. A horrible, ugly, snotty creature was stretched out under a duvet in the comfy black chair. Horrid Henry glanced at the TV. A dreadful assortment of wobbling creatures were dancing and prancing.

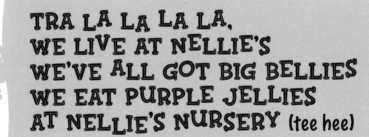

TRA LA LA LA LA,
WE LIVE AT NELLIE'S
WE'VE ALL GOT BIG BELLIES
WE EAT PURPLE JELLIES
AT NELLIE'S NURSERY (tee hee)

Horrid Henry sat down on the sofa.

'I want to watch *Robot Rebels*,' said Henry.

'I'm watching *Nellie's Nursery*,' said Peter, sniffing.

'Stop sniffing,' said Henry.

'I can't help it, my nose is running,' said Peter.

'I'm sicker than you, and *I'm* not sniffing,' said Henry.

'I'm sicker than you,' said Peter.

'Faker.'

'Faker.'

'Liar.'

'Liar!'

'MUM!' shrieked Henry and Peter.

Mum came into the room, carrying a tray of cold drinks and two thermometers.

'Henry's being mean to me!' whined Peter.

'Peter's being mean to *me*!' whined Henry.

'If you're well enough to fight, you're well enough to go to school, Henry,' said Mum, glaring at him.

'I wasn't fighting, Peter was,' said Henry.

'Henry was,' said Peter, coughing.

Henry coughed louder.

Peter groaned.

Henry groaned louder.

'Uggghhhhh,' moaned Peter.

'Uggghhhhhhhhh,' moaned Henry. 'It's not fair. I want to watch *Robot Rebels*.'

'I want to watch *Nellie's Nursery*,' whimpered Peter.

'Peter will choose what to watch because he's the sickest,' said Mum.

Peter, sicker than he was? As if. Well, no way was Henry's sick day going to be ruined by his horrible brother.

'I'm the sickest, Mum,' protested Henry. 'I just don't complain so much.'

Mum looked tired. She popped one thermometer into Henry's mouth and the other into Peter's.

'I'll be back in five minutes to check them,' she said. 'And I don't want to hear another peep from either of you,' she added, leaving the room.

Horrid Henry lay back weakly on the sofa with the thermometer in his mouth. He felt terrible. He touched his forehead. He was burning! His temperature must be 45!

I bet my temperature is so high the thermometer won't even have enough numbers, thought Henry. Just wait till Mum saw how ill he was. Then she'd be sorry she'd been so mean.

Perfect Peter started groaning. 'I'm going to be sick,' he gasped, taking the thermometer from his mouth and running from the room.

The moment Peter left, Henry leapt up from the sofa and checked Peter's thermometer. 39 degrees! Oh no, Peter had a temperature. Now Peter would start getting *all* the attention. Mum would make Henry fetch and carry for him. Peter might even get extra ice cream.

Something had to be done.

Quickly Henry plunged Peter's thermometer into the glass of iced water.

Beep. Beep. Horrid Henry took out his own thermometer. It read 37.5C. Normal.

Normal! His temperature was normal? That was impossible. How could his temperature be normal when he was so ill?

If Mum saw that normal temperature she'd have him dressed for school in three seconds. Obviously there was something wrong with that stupid thermometer.

Horrid Henry held it to the light bulb. Just to warm it up a little, he thought.

Clump. Clump.

Yikes! Mum was coming back.

Quickly Henry yanked Peter's thermometer out of the iced water and replaced his own in his mouth. Oww! It was hot.

'Let's see if you have a temperature,' said Mum. She took the thermometer out of Henry's mouth.

'50 degrees!' she shrieked.

Oops.

'The thermometer must be broken,' mumbled Henry. 'But I still have a temperature. I'm boiling.'

'Hmmn,' said Mum, feeling Henry's forehead.

Peter came back into the sitting room slowly. His face was ashen.

'Check *my* temperature, Mum,' said Peter. He lay back weakly on the pillows.

Mum checked Peter's thermometer.

'10 degrees!' she shrieked.

Oops, thought Horrid Henry.

'That one must be broken too,' said Henry.

He decided to change the subject fast.

'Mum, could you open the curtains please?' said Henry.

'But I want them closed,' said Peter.

'Open!'

'Closed!'

'We'll leave them closed,' said Mum.

Peter sneezed.

'Mum!' wailed Henry. 'Peter got snot all over me.'

'Mum!' wailed Peter. 'Henry's smelly.'

Horrid Henry glared at Peter.

Perfect Peter glared at Henry.

Henry whistled.

Peter hummed.

'Henry's whistling!'

'Peter's humming!'

'MUM!' they screamed. 'Make him stop!'

'That's enough!' shouted Mum. 'Go to your bedrooms, both of you!'

Henry and Peter heaved their heavy bones upstairs to their rooms.

'It's all your fault,' said Henry.

'It's yours,' said Peter.

The front door opened. Dad came in. He looked pale.

'I'm not feeling well,' said Dad. 'I'm going to bed.'

Horrid Henry was bored. Horrid Henry was fed up. What was the point of being sick if you couldn't watch TV and you couldn't play on the computer?

'I'm hungry!' complained Horrid Henry.

'I'm thirsty,' complained Perfect Peter.

'I'm achy,' complained Dad.

'My bed's too hot!' moaned Horrid Henry.

'My bed's too cold,' moaned Perfect Peter.

'My bed's too hot and too cold,' moaned Dad.

Mum ran up the stairs.

Mum ran down the stairs.

'Ice cream!' shouted Horrid Henry.

'Hot water bottle!' shouted Perfect Peter.

'More pillows!' shouted Dad.

Mum walked up the stairs.

Mum walked down the stairs.

'Toast!' shouted Henry.

'Tissues!' croaked Peter.

'Tea!' gasped Dad.

'Can you wait a minute?' said Mum. 'I need to sit down.'

'NO!' shouted Henry, Peter, and Dad.

'All right,' said Mum.

She plodded up the stairs.

She plodded down the stairs.

'My head is hurting!'

'My throat is hurting!'

'My stomach is hurting!'

Mum trudged up the stairs.

Mum trudged down the stairs.

'Crisps,' screeched Henry.

'Throat lozenge,' croaked Peter.

'Hankie,' wheezed Dad.

Mum staggered up the stairs.

Mum staggered down the stairs.

Then Horrid Henry saw the time. Three-thirty. School was finished! The weekend was here! It was amazing, thought Horrid Henry, how much better he suddenly felt.

Horrid Henry threw off his duvet and leapt out of bed.

'Mum!' he shouted. 'I'm feeling much better. Can I go and play on the computer now?'

Mum staggered into his room.

'Thank goodness you're better, Henry,' she whispered. 'I feel terrible. I'm going to bed. Could you bring me a cup of tea?'

What?

'I'm busy,' snapped Henry.

Mum glared at him.

'All right,' said Henry, grudgingly. Why couldn't Mum get her own tea? She had legs, didn't she?

Horrid Henry escaped into the sitting room. He sat down at the computer and loaded 'Intergalactic Robot Rebellion: This Time It's Personal'. Bliss. He'd zap some robots, then have a go at 'Snake Master's Revenge'.

'Henry!' gasped Mum. 'Where's my tea?'

'Henry!' rasped Dad. 'Bring me a drink of water!'

'Henry!' whimpered Peter. 'Bring me an extra blanket.'

Horrid Henry scowled. Honestly, how was he meant to concentrate with all these interruptions?

'Tea!'

'Water!'

'Blanket!'

'Get it yourself!' he howled. What was he, a servant?

'Henry!' spluttered Dad. 'Come up here this minute.'

Slowly, Horrid Henry got to his feet. He looked longingly at the flashing screen. But what choice did he have?

'I'm sick too!' shrieked Horrid Henry. 'I'm going back to bed.'

Dear Miss Battle-Axe
Henry cudn't come to school
Yesterday because a wirwolf
bit him.
Yours sincerly
Henry's mum.

Dear Mis Battle-Axe
Henry has the black plage
So he can't take his maths
test today or do P.E.
The docter says doing any
home work cud be DEADLY

Yours Sincerly
Henrys mum.

Dear Mis Battle-Axe
Henry was sik yesterday with
a temprature of 52C. He
was so hot he set fire to his
bed which burned his room wich
ment he had no clothes to wear.
Yours Sincerly
Henry's Mum

HORRID HENRY
PEEKS AT
PETER'S DIARY

'What are you doing?' demanded Horrid Henry, bursting into Peter's bedroom.

'Nothing,' said Perfect Peter quickly, slamming his notebook shut.

'Yes you are,' said Henry.

'Get out of my room,' said Peter. 'You're not allowed to come in unless I say so.'

Horrid Henry leaned over Peter's shoulder.

'What are you writing?'

'None of your business,' said Peter. He covered the closed notebook tightly with his arm.

'It is *too* my business if you're writing about *me*.'

'It's *my* diary. I can write what I want to,' said Peter. 'Miss Lovely said we should keep a diary for a week and write in it every day.'

'Bo-ring,' said Henry, yawning.

'No it isn't,' said Peter. 'Anyway, you'll find out next week what I'm writing: I've been chosen to read my diary out loud for our class assembly.'

Horrid Henry's heart turned to ice.

Peter read his diary out loud? So the whole school could hear Peter's lies about him? No way!

'Gimme that!' screamed Horid Henry, lunging for the diary.

'No!' screamed Peter, holding on tight. 'MUUUM! Help! Henry's in my room! And he didn't knock!

And he won't leave!'

'Shut up, tattle-tale,' hissed Henry, forcing Peter's fingers off the diary.

'MUUUUMMMMMM!' shrieked Peter.

Mum stomped up the stairs.

Henry opened the diary. But before he could read a single word Mum burst in.

'He snatched my diary! And he told me to shut up!' wailed Peter.

'Henry! Stop annoying your brother,' said Mum.

'I wasn't,' said Henry.

'Yes he was,' snivelled Peter.

'And now you've made him cry,' said Mum. 'Say sorry.'

'I was just asking about his homework,' protested Henry innocently.

'He was trying to read my diary,' said Peter.

'Henry!' said Mum. 'Don't be horrid. A diary is private. Now leave your brother alone.'

It was so unfair. Why did Mum always believe Peter?

Humph. Horrid Henry stalked out of Peter's bedroom. Well, no way was Henry waiting until class assembly to find out what Peter had written.

Horrid Henry checked to the right. Horrid Henry checked to the left. Mum was downstairs working on the computer. Dad was in the garden. Peter was playing at Goody-Goody Gordon's house.

At last, the coast was clear. He'd been trying to get hold of Peter's diary for days. There was no time to lose.

Tomorrow was Peter's class assembly. Would he mention Sunday's food fight, when Henry had been forced to throw soggy pasta at Peter? Or when Henry had to push Peter off the comfy black chair and pinch him? Or yesterday when Henry banished him from the Purple Hand Club and Peter had run screaming to Mum? A lying, slimy worm like Peter would be sure to make it look like Henry was the villain when in fact Peter was always to blame.

Even worse, what horrid lies had Peter been making up about him? People would read Peter's ravings and think they were true. When Henry was famous, books would be written about him, and someone would find Peter's diary and believe it! When things were written down they had a horrible way of seeming to be true even when they were big fat lies.

Henry sneaked into Peter's bedroom and shut the door. Now, where was that diary? Henry glanced at Peter's tidy desk. Peter kept it on the second shelf, next to his crayons and trophies.

The diary was gone.

Rats. Peter must have hidden it.

That little worm, thought Horrid Henry. Why on earth would he hide his diary? And *where* on earth would that smelly toad hide it? Behind his 'Good as Gold' certificates? In the laundry basket? Underneath his stamp collection?

He checked Peter's sock drawer. No diary.

He checked Peter's underwear drawer. No diary.

He peeked under Peter's pillow, and under Peter's bed. Still no diary.

OK, where would *I* hide a diary, thought Horrid Henry desperately. Easy. I'd put it in a chest and bury it in the garden, with a pirate curse on it.

Somehow he doubted Perfect Peter would be so clever.

OK, thought Henry, if I were an ugly toad like him, where would I hide it?

The bookcase. Of course. What better place to hide a book?

Henry strolled over to Peter's bookcase, with all the books arranged neatly in alphabetical order. Aha! What was that sticking out between *The Happy Nappy* and *The Hoppy Hippo*?

Gotcha, thought Horrid Henry, yanking the diary off the shelf. At last he would know Peter's secrets.

He'd make him cross out all his lies if it was the last thing he did.

Horrid Henry sat down and began to read:

Monday
Today I drew a picture of my teacher, Miss Lovely. Miss Lovely gave me a gold star for reading. That's because I'm the best reader in the class. And the best at maths. And the best at everything else.

Tuesday
Today I said please and thank you 236 times

Wednesday
Today I ate all my vegetables

> Thursday
> Today I sharpened my pencils.
> I ate all my sprouts and had
> seconds.
>
> Friday
> Today I wrote a poem to my mummy
> I Love my mummy,
> I came out of her tummy,
> Her food is yummy,
> She is so scrummy,
> I love my mummy.

Slowly Horrid Henry closed Peter's diary. He knew Peter's diary would be bad. But never in his worst nightmares had he imagined anything this bad.

Perfect Peter hadn't mentioned him once. Not once.

You'd think I didn't even live in this house, thought Henry. He was outraged. How dare Peter *not* write about him? And then all the stupid things Peter *had* written.

Henry's name would be mud when people heard

Peter's diary in assembly and found out what a sad brother he had. Everyone would tease him. Horrid Henry would never live down the shame.

Peter needed Henry's help, and he needed it fast. Horrid Henry grabbed a pencil and got to work.

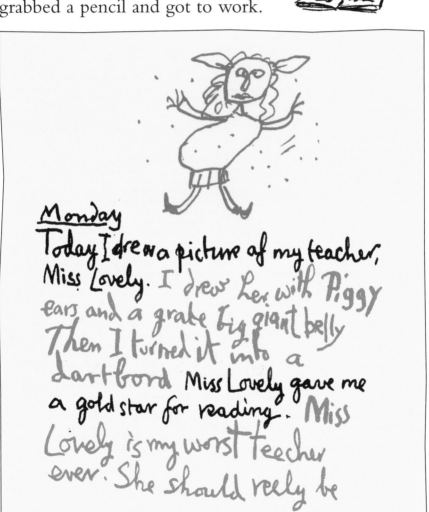

<u>Monday</u>
Today I drew a picture of my teacher, Miss Lovely. I drew her with Piggy ears and a grate big giant belly Then I turned it into a dartbord Miss Lovely gave me a gold star for reading. Miss Lovely is my worst teacher ever. She should reely be

Called Miss Lumpy.
Miss Dumpy Lumpy is wot Gordon
and I call her behind her back.
Tee hee, she'll never know!

I'm the best reader in the class. And
the best at maths. And the best at
everything else. Too bad I have
smelly pants and nitty hair

That's more like it, thought Horrid Henry.

Tuesday
Today I said please and thank you
236 times

~~Not!~~ Not! I called Mum a big
blobby pants face. I called Dad
a stinky fish. Then I played
Pirats with the worlds greatest
brother, Henry. I wish I were as

clever as Henry. But I know
that's imposibel.

Wednesday
Today I ate all my vegetables

then I sneeked loads of sweets from
the sweet Jar ⬚⬚⬚ and
lied to dad about it. I am
a very good liar. No one should
ever beleeve a word I say.
Henry gets the blame but reely
every thing is always my fault.

Thursday
Today I sharpened my pencils.
All the better to write rude notes!

I ate all my sprouts and had
Seconds. Then threw up all over
Mum. Eeugh, what a Smell. I
reelly am a smelly toad. I am
So lucky to have a grate brother
like Henry. He is always so nice to me
Hip Hip Hurray for Henry

Friday
Today I wrote a poem to my Dummy
    I Love my Dummy,
    It's my best chummy
    It tastes So yummy,
    It is so Scrummy,
    I love my Dummy.

Much better, thought Horrid Henry. Now that's
what I call a diary. Everyone would have died of
boredom otherwise.

Henry carefully replaced Peter's diary in the bookcase. I hope Peter appreciates what I've done for him, thought Horrid Henry.

The entire school gathered in the hall for assembly. Peter's class sat proudly on benches at the front. Henry's class sat cross-legged on the floor. The parents sat on chairs down both sides.

Mum and Dad waved at Peter. He waved shyly back. Miss Lovely stood up.

'Hello Mums and Dads, boys and girls, welcome to our class assembly. This term our class has been keeping diaries. We're going to read some of them to you now. First to read will be Peter. Everyone pay attention, and see if you too can be as good as I know Peter has been. I'd like everyone here to copy one of Peter's good deeds. I know I can't wait to hear how he has spent this last week.'

Peter stood up, and opened his diary. In a big loud voice, he read:

MONDAY

'Today I drew a picture of my teacher, Miss Lovely.' Peter glanced up at Miss Lovely. She beamed at him.

'I drew her with piggy ears and a great big giant belly. Then I turned it into a dartboard.'

What??! It was always difficult to read out loud and understand what he had read, but something didn't sound right. He didn't remember writing about a pig with a big belly. Nervously Peter looked up at Mum and Dad. Was he imagining it, or did their smiles seem more like frowns? Peter shook his head, and carried on.

'Miss Lovely gave me a gold star for reading.'

Phew, that was better! He must have misheard himself before.

'Miss Lovely is my worst teacher ever. She should really be called Miss Lumpy. Miss Dumpy Lumpy—'

'Thank you, that's quite
enough,' interrupted
Miss Lovely sternly, as
the school erupted in
shrieks of laughter.
Her face was pink.
'Peter, see me after
assembly. Ted will
now tell us all about
skeletons.'

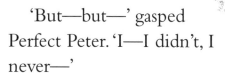

'But—but—' gasped
Perfect Peter. 'I—I didn't, I
never—'

'Sit down and be quiet,' said the head, Mrs Oddbod.
'I'll see you *and* your parents later.'

'WAAAAAAAAA!' wailed Peter.

Mum and Dad stared at their feet. Why had they
ever had children? Where was a trapdoor when you
needed one?

'Waaaaaaaa,' whimpered Mum and Dad.

Naturally, Henry got into trouble. Big big trouble. It was so unfair. Why didn't anyone believe him when he said he'd improved Peter's diary for his own good? Honestly, he would never *ever* do Peter a favour again.

HORRID HENRY'S DIARY

MONDAY Today I wrot Magaret a pome. I can't beleeve she didnt like it (tee hee). I swiped ~~Peters~~ 5 chips off Peters plate when he wasn't looking, and sneaked all my peas on to his !!!

TUESDAY Today I hid a Mad Max comick inside my maths book during class. Unfortunatly, I forgot to check that my maths book was the rite way up — Woops! ∽∽∽

WEDNESDAY Great day! I found 50p on the street and bougt a huge bar of chocolit !!!

THURSDAY Mum wouldn't let me wach extra T.V. so I called her a stinky fish. Well she is. Then Dad wouldn't let me have more crisps, so I called him a big blobby pants face delux. Now I am in my room.

FRIDAY Peter tried to grab the cumfy black chair but I tricked him by telling him that Mum was calling him. Then I nabbed it. A perfick start to the weakend !!!

HORRID HENRY'S CHRISTMAS PLAY

A COLD DARK DAY in NOVEMBER
(37 days till Christmas)

Horrid Henry slumped on the carpet and willed the clock to go faster. Only five more minutes to hometime! Already Henry could taste those crisps he'd be sneaking from the cupboard.

Miss Battle-Axe droned on about school dinners (yuck), the new drinking fountain blah blah blah, maths homework blah blah blah, the school Christmas play blah blah . . . what? Did Miss Battle-Axe say . . . Christmas play? Horrid Henry sat up.

'This is a brand-new play with singing and dancing,' continued Miss Battle-Axe. 'And both the older and the younger children are taking part this year.'

Singing! Dancing! Showing off in front of the whole school! Years ago, when Henry was in the infants' class, he'd played eighth sheep in the nativity play and had snatched the baby from the manger and refused

170

to hand him back. Henry hoped Miss Battle-Axe
wouldn't remember.

Because Henry had to play the lead. He had to.
Who else but Henry could be an all-singing, all-dancing
Joseph?

'I want to be Mary,' shouted every girl in the class.

'I want to be a wise man!' shouted Rude Ralph.

'I want to be a sheep!' shouted Anxious Andrew.

'I want to be Joseph!' shouted Horrid Henry.

'No, me!' shouted Jazzy Jim.

'Me!' shouted Brainy Brian.

'Quiet!' shrieked Miss Battle-Axe. 'I'm the director,
and my decision about who will act which part is
final. I've cast the play as follows: Margaret. You will be
Mary.' She handed her a thick script.

Moody Margaret whooped with joy. All the other
girls glared at her.

'Susan, front legs of the donkey; Linda, hind legs;
cows, Fiona and Clare. Blades of grass—' Miss Battle-Axe
continued assigning parts.

Pick me for Joseph, pick me
for Joseph, Horrid Henry
begged silently. Who better than
the best actor in the school to
play the starring part?

'I'm a sheep, I'm a sheep, I'm a beautiful
sheep!' warbled Singing Soraya.

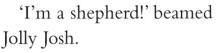

'I'm a shepherd!' beamed Jolly Josh.

'I'm an angel,' trilled Magic Martha.

'I'm a blade of grass,' sobbed Weepy William.

'Joseph will be played by—'

'ME!' screamed Henry.

'Me!' screamed New Nick, Greedy Graham, Dizzy Dave and Aerobic Al.

'—Peter,' said Miss Battle-Axe. 'From Miss Lovely's class.'

Horrid Henry felt as if he'd been slugged in the stomach. Perfect Peter? His *younger* brother? Perfect Peter get the starring part?

'It's not fair!' howled Horrid Henry.

Miss Battle-Axe glared at him.

'Henry, you're—' Miss Battle-Axe consulted her list. Please not a blade of grass, please not a blade of grass, prayed Horrid Henry, shrinking. That would be just like Miss Battle-Axe, to humiliate him. Anything but that—

'—the innkeeper.'

The innkeeper! Horrid Henry sat up, beaming. How stupid he'd been: the *innkeeper* must be the starring part. Henry could see himself now, polishing glasses, throwing darts, pouring out big foaming Fizzywizz drinks to all his happy customers while singing a song about the joys of innkeeping. Then he'd get into a nice long argument about why there was no room at the inn, and finally, the chance to slam the door in Moody Margaret's face after he'd pushed her away. Wow. Maybe he'd even get a second song. 'Ten Green Bottles' would fit right into the story: he'd sing and dance while knocking his less talented classmates off a wall. Wouldn't that be fun!

Miss Battle-Axe handed a page to Henry. 'Your script,' she said.

Henry was puzzled. Surely there were some pages missing?

He read:

(Joseph knocks. The innkeeper opens the door.)

JOSEPH: Is there any room at the inn?
INNKEEPER: No.

(The innkeeper shuts the door.)

Horrid Henry turned over the page.

It was blank. He held it up to the light.

There was no secret writing. That was it.

His entire part was one line. One stupid puny line. Not even a line, a word. 'No.'

Where was his song? Where was his dance with the bottles and the guests at the inn? How could he, Horrid Henry, the best actor in the class (and indeed, the world) be given just one word in the school play? Even the donkeys got a song.

Worse, after he said his *one* word, Perfect Peter and Moody Margaret got to yack for hours about mangers and wise men and shepherds and sheep, and then sing a duet, while he, Henry, hung about behind the hay with the blades of grass.

It was so unfair!

He should be the star of the show, not his stupid worm of a brother. Why on earth was Peter cast as

Joseph anyway? He was a terrible actor. He couldn't sing, he just squeaked like a squished toad. And why was Margaret playing Mary? Now she'd never stop bragging and swaggering.

AAARRRRGGGGHHHH!

'Isn't it exciting!' said Mum.

'Isn't it thrilling!' said Dad. 'Our little boy, the star of the show.'

'Well done, Peter,' said Mum.

'We're so proud of you,' said Dad.

Perfect Peter smiled modestly.

'Of course I'm not *really* the star,' he said, 'Everyone's important, even little parts like the blades of grass and the innkeeper.'

Horrid Henry pounced. He was a Great White shark lunging for the kill.

squealed Peter. 'Henry bit me!'

'Henry! Don't be horrid!' snapped Mum.

'Henry! Go to your room!' snapped Dad.

Horrid Henry stomped upstairs and slammed the door. How could he bear the humiliation of playing the innkeeper when Peter was the star? He'd just have to force Peter to switch roles with him. Henry was sure he could find a way to persuade Peter, but persuading Miss Battle-Axe was a different matter. Miss Battle-Axe had a mean, horrible way of never doing what Henry wanted.

Maybe he could trick Peter into leaving the show. Yes! And then nobly offer to replace him.

But unfortunately, there was no guarantee Miss Battle-Axe would give Henry Peter's role. She'd probably just replace Peter with Goody-Goody Gordon. He was stuck.

And then Horrid Henry had a brilliant, spectacular idea. Why hadn't he thought of this before? If he couldn't play a bigger part, he'd just have to make his part bigger. For instance, he could *scream* 'No.' *That* would get a reaction. Or he could bellow 'No,' and then hit Joseph. I'm an angry innkeeper, thought Horrid Henry, and I hate guests coming to my inn. Certainly smelly ones like Joseph. Or he could shout 'No!', hit Joseph, then rob him. I'm a robber innkeeper, thought Henry. Or, I'm a robber *pretending* to be an innkeeper. That would liven up the play a bit. Maybe he could be a French robber innkeeper, shout '*Non*', and rob Mary and Joseph. Or he was a French robber *pirate* innkeeper, so he could shout '*Non*,' tie Mary and Joseph up and make them walk the plank. Hmmm, thought Horrid Henry. Maybe my part won't be so small. After all, the innkeeper *was* the most important character.

12 December
(only 13 more days till Christmas)

Rehearsals had been going on forever. Horrid Henry spent most of his time slumping in a chair. He'd never seen such a boring play. Naturally he'd done everything he could to improve it.

'Can't I add a dance?' asked Henry.

'No,' snapped Miss Battle-Axe.

'Can't I add a teeny-weeny little song?' Henry pleaded.

'No!' said Miss Battle-Axe.

'But how does the innkeeper *know* there's no room?' said Henry. 'I think I should—'

Miss Battle-Axe glared at him with her red eyes.

'One more word from you, Henry, and you'll change places with Linda,' snapped Miss Battle-Axe. 'Blades of grass, let's try again . . .'

178

Eeek! An innkeeper with one word was infinitely better than being invisible as the hind legs of a donkey. Still—it was so unfair. He was only trying to help.

22 DECEMBER (only 3 more days till Christmas!)

Showtime! Not a teatowel was to be found in any local shop. Mums and dads had been up all night frantically sewing costumes. Now the waiting and the rehearsing were over.

Everyone lined up on stage behind the curtain. Peter and Margaret waited on the side to make their big entrance as Mary and Joseph.

'Isn't it exciting, Henry, being in a real play?' whispered Peter.

'NO,' snarled Henry.

'Places, everyone, for the opening song,' hissed Miss Battle-Axe. 'Now remember, don't worry if you make a little mistake: just carry on and no one will notice.'

'But I still think I should have an argument with

Mary and Joseph about whether there's room,' said
Henry. 'Shouldn't I at least check to see—'

'No!' snapped Miss Battle-Axe, glaring at him. 'If I
hear another peep from you, Henry, you will sit behind
the bales of hay and Jim will play your part. Blades of
grass! Line up with the donkeys! Sheep! Get ready to
baaa . . . Bert! Are you a sheep or a blade of grass?'

'I dunno,' said Beefy Bert.

Mrs Oddbod went to the front of the stage.
'Welcome everyone, mums and dads, boys and girls, to
our new Christmas play, a little different from previous
years. We hope you all enjoy a brand new show!'

Miss Battle-Axe started the CD player. The music pealed. The curtain rose. The audience stamped and cheered. Stars twinkled. Cows mooed. Horses neighed. Sheep baa'ed. Cameras flashed.

Horrid Henry stood in the wings and watched the shepherds do their Highland dance. He still hadn't decided for sure how he was going to play his part. There were so many possibilities. It was so hard to choose.

Finally, Henry's big moment arrived.

He strode across the stage and waited behind the closed inn door for Mary and Joseph.

Knock! Knock! Knock!

The innkeeper stepped forward and opened the door. There was Moody Margaret, simpering away as Mary, and Perfect Peter looking full of himself as Joseph.

'Is there any room at the inn?' asked Joseph.

Good question, thought Horrid Henry. His mind was blank. He'd thought of so many great things he *could* say that what he was *supposed* to say had just gone straight out of his head.

'Is there any room at the inn?' repeated Joseph loudly.

'Yes,' said the innkeeper. 'Come on in.'

Joseph looked at Mary.

Mary looked at Joseph.

The audience murmured.

Oops, thought Horrid Henry. Now he remembered. He'd been supposed to say no. Oh well, in for a penny, in for a pound.

The innkeeper grabbed Mary and Joseph's sleeves and yanked them through the door. 'Come on in, I haven't got all day.'

' . . . but . . . but . . . the inn's *full*,' said Mary.

'No it isn't,' said the innkeeper.

'Is too.'

'Is not. It's my inn and I should know. This is the best inn in Bethlehem, we've got TVs and beds, and—' the innkeeper paused for a moment. What *did* inns have in them? '—and computers!'

Mary glared at the innkeeper.

The innkeeper glared at Mary.

Miss Battle-Axe gestured frantically from the wings.

'This inn looks full to me,' said Mary firmly. 'Come on Joseph, let's go to the stable.'

'Oh, don't go there, you'll get fleas,' said the innkeeper.

'So?' said Mary.

'I love fleas,' said Joseph weakly.

'And it's full of manure.'

'So are you,' snapped Mary.

'Don't be horrid, Mary,' said the innkeeper severely. 'Now sit down and rest your weary bones and I'll sing ou a song.' And the innkeeper started singing:

'**Ten green bottles, standing on a wall**
Ten green bottles, standing on a wall,
And if one green bottle should accidentally
    fall—

'Ooohhh!'

moaned Mary. 'I'm having the baby.'

'Can't you wait till I've finished my song?' snapped the inkeeper.

'NO!' bellowed Mary.

Miss Battle-Axe drew her hand across her throat.

Henry ignored her. After all, the show must go on.

'Come on, Joseph,' interrupted Mary. 'We're going to the stable.'

'OK,' said Joseph.

'You're making a big mistake,' said the innkeeper. 'We've got satellite TV and . . . '

Miss Battle-Axe ran on stage and nabbed him.

'Thank you, innkeeper, your other guests need you now,' said Miss Battle-Axe, grabbing him by the collar.

'Merry Christmas!' shrieked Horrid Henry as she yanked him off-stage.

There was a very long silence.

'Bravo!' yelled Moody Margaret's deaf aunt.

Mum and Dad weren't sure what to do. Should they clap, or run away to a place where no one knew them?

Mum clapped.

Dad hid his face in his hands.

'Do you think anyone noticed?' whispered Mum.

Dad looked at Mrs Oddbod's grim face. He sank down in his chair. Maybe one day he would learn how to make himself invisible.

'But what was I *supposed* to do?' said Horrid Henry afterwards in Mrs Oddbod's office. 'It's not *my* fault I forgot my line. Miss Battle-Axe said not to worry if we made a mistake and just to carry on.'

Could he help it if a star was born?

KING HENRY THE HORRIBLE'S FACT FILE

* *

Worst subjects

Miss Battle-Axe
Moody Margaret
Stuck-up Steve
Perfect Peter
Mrs Oddbod

* *

Best banquet

To start:
Chocolate
    yum-yums

Main courses:
Pizza
Burgers
Chips
Chocolate

Desserts:
Chocolate ice cream
Chocolate cake
Chocolate biscuits
Fudge

Worst banquet

Chef had his head chopped off

To start: Spinach tart

Main courses:

Mussels
Tripe

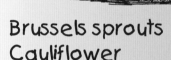

Dessert:
Fresh fruit

Brussels sprouts
Cauliflower

Ugh!

Best punishments

Piranha-infested moat
Snakepit
Man-eating crocodiles
Scorpion cage

* *

Best law

Parents have to go to school, not children

* *

Worst crimes

Saying the word 'chores'
Setting homework
Bedtime

* *

Best throne

Comfy black chair

* * * * * * * * * * * * * * * * * * * *

Worst throne

School chair

* *

Best regal robes

Terminator Gladiator
dressing-gown

* * * * * * * * * * * * * * * * * * * *

Worst regal robes

Pageboy outfit

* * * * * * * * * * * * * * * * * * *

Best palace

300 rooms with 300 TVs

HORRID HENRY
by Francesca Simon
Illustrated by Tony Ross

Paperbacks with four stories each

HORRID HENRY
HORRID HENRY AND THE SECRET CLUB
HORRID HENRY TRICKS THE TOOTH FAIRY
HORRID HENRY'S NITS
HORRID HENRY GETS RICH QUICK
HORRID HENRY'S REVENGE
HORRID HENRY'S HAUNTED HOUSE
HORRID HENRY AND THE MUMMY'S CURSE
HORRID HENRY AND THE BOGEY BABYSITTER
HORRID HENRY'S STINKBOMB
HORRID HENRY'S UNDERPANTS
HORRID HENRY MEETS THE QUEEN
HORRID HENRY AND THE MEGA-MEAN TIME MACHINE
HORRID HENRY AND THE FOOTBALL FIEND
HORRID HENRY'S CHRISTMAS CRACKER
HORRID HENRY AND THE ABOMINABLE SNOWMAN

Big colour collections of stories from the paperbacks

HORRID HENRY'S BIG BAD BOOK
HORRID HENRY'S EVIL ENEMIES
HORRID HENRY'S WICKED WAYS

Extra books

HORRID HENRY'S JOKE BOOK
HORRID HENRY'S JOLLY JOKE BOOK

All the storybooks are available on audio cassette
and CD, read by Miranda Richardson